KILL ONLY LESSER MEN

DISILLUSIONED WITH HIS CHURCH AND ANGRY WITH GOD, ANTHONY MARTINO WAS FREED FROM THE MORAL CHAINS THAT ONCE RESTRAINED HIS MURDEROUS WAYS

ART MARSICANO

Author of Some Men Need Killing

KILL ONLY LESSER MEN
DISILLUSIONED WITH HIS CHURCH AND ANGRY WITH
GOD, ANTHONY MARTINO WAS FREED FROM THE MORAL
CHAINS THAT ONCE RESTRAINED HIS MURDEROUS WAYS

This is a work of fiction. All of the characters, names, incidents, organizations, and dialogue
in this novel are either the products of the author's imagination or are used fictitiously.

iUniverse books may be ordered through booksellers or by contacting:

iUniverse
1663 Liberty Drive
Bloomington, IN 47403
www.iuniverse.com
1-800-Authors (1-800-288-4677)

Because of the dynamic nature of the Internet, any web addresses or links contained in
this book may have changed since publication and may no longer be valid. The views
expressed in this work are solely those of the author and do not necessarily reflect the
views of the publisher, and the publisher hereby disclaims any responsibility for them.

Any people depicted in stock imagery provided by Thinkstock are models,
and such images are being used for illustrative purposes only.
Certain stock imagery © Thinkstock.

ISBN: 978-1-5320-3205-9 (sc)
ISBN: 978-1-5320-3207-3 (hc)
ISBN: 978-1-5320-3206-6 (e)

Library of Congress Control Number: 2017913486

Print information available on the last page.

iUniverse rev. date: 10/06/2017

ALSO BY ART MARSICANO

The Last Two Years (2006)

Some Men Need Killing (2008)

Laugh at the Devil (2009)

Nowhere … a Region of Uncertainty in the Afterworld (2012)

A Place in My Mind (2015)

DEDICATION

To the Irish and Italian immigrants who came to the United States to build a better life for themselves and their families. They had much in common including the many injustices they faced, their love of church and family, and histories filled with violence and conflict that continued for years after their arrival—frequently with each other.

PROLOGUE

This novel is a work of fiction inspired by events that took place in the northeastern part of the United States during the 1960s and 70s. The main characters are from New York City and the anthracite region of Pennsylvania—*hard coal country*. Others are from the Boston area.

Recorded history contains errors, inconsistencies and obvious gaps. This is especially so when powerful and ruthless men control events that impact large numbers of people, even nations. Perhaps fiction is the best way to complete the story when history fails us. Good fiction built on logic and what is known may be better than an incomplete or incorrect historical record. And so, this novel is a work of fiction, yet portions of it are based on important events that were never adequately explained. Parts of this book were inspired by events that took place in Pennsylvania, especially in its anthracite region. However, in this book the Italian criminals of the anthracite region find themselves involved in a crime war that has raged in the United States between the Italians and the Irish for nearly a century. Their conflict continued until very recently and may still smolder, just out of view. Law enforcement agencies were often involved in the conflict, usually on the side of the Irish. In the Boston area, for example, there is little doubt that the FBI cooperated with Irish mobsters while allowing innocent Italians to be convicted of serious crimes they did not commit.

Pennsylvania has a long tradition of crime and corruption extending to elected officials, police officers and the legal profession, including judges. Although it was true throughout the state, it was especially common in areas where Italian criminal organizations existed, particularly the Philadelphia and Pittsburgh areas, and the eight northeastern counties where anthracite, commonly known as hard coal, is found. In *hard coal country* a triangle of crime and moral corruption involving the criminal justice system, the Roman Catholic Church and criminals existed for more than 150 years. It should be noted that each side had friends and enemies within the other two adding many layers of confusion to the historical record. It was true in the 1960s and 70s, the period in which this and the two previous novels I wrote about Italian criminals took place, and to some extent it remains true today.

The federal government has intervened many times when Pennsylvania's judges, law enforcement personnel and politicians have descended too deeply into the dark abyss of crime and corruption. Yet who sees to it that the federal government is behaving properly?

The federal government gave the nation the Vietnam War, largely under Presidents Kennedy and Johnson, in which more than 50,000 Americans died in a war which should not have been fought and could not be won; a deadly assault on a compound in Waco, Texas in 1993, justified in part as an effort to protect children, which resulted in the deaths of seventy-six people including more than twenty children and two pregnant women; and more than four hundred failed attempts to assassinate Fidel Castro, some with the help of the Mafia. Federal law enforcement officials have also engaged in aggressive illegal behavior in combating crime. Federal authorities and agencies are clearly better than local and state police when it comes to concealing their indiscretions.

In 1965 Edward Diegan was murdered and four men were sent to prison for a crime the FBI knew they did not commit! In fact, the FBI was involved in the frame-up of the innocent men. The cover up continued for nearly 40 years. When the illegal FBI conduct surfaced, the surviving innocent men were released and a lawsuit was filed against the federal government. In 2003 the federal Judge in charge of the case, Nancy Gertover, said "The FBI's misconduct was clearly the sole cause of the conviction." The four men served a total of 109 years in prison and two of them died there. The Judge ordered the government to pay a record $101.7 million to the families of the four men, including the two who survived more than three decades in prison. During the legal proceedings, the FBI argued that it was not obligated to share information with state prosecutors. That lame excuse was an attempt to mask a far more sinister motive. FBI agents in New England had been in bed with Irish mobsters of Boston for many years, and they clearly preferred to convict innocent Italian Americans who may have been connected with the Italian mob in minor roles, rather than Irish criminals who had murdered more than a few times. Indeed, it is widely believed that an FBI agent helped the head of the Irish mob avoid capture. The same agent very likely helped set up several killings by the Irish mob.

During the 1960s, the FBI seemingly made a conscious effort to become involved in the war between the Irish and Italian criminal organizations. Certainly not all did, but at least some FBI agents in the Boston area helped the Irish criminals while allowing innocent Italian Americans to be convicted of murder! Why? Could it possibly have been related to the assassination of President Kennedy in 1963, an Irish American from the Boston area who many believe was killed by the Italian mob, not by a lone shooter, Lee Harvey Oswald.

It is well documented that the Italian mob played a critical role in helping John Kennedy become the 35th President of the United States. Once elected, however, the President's brother, Robert Kennedy, aggressively went after "organized" Italian criminals. People who believe that the Italian mob was responsible for killing President Kennedy are often depicted as conspiracy nuts or worse. Yet none other than Robert Kennedy, who was the attorney general at the time of his brother's assassination, believed the Italian mob killed his brother. In fact, he hoped to one day become President of the United States and reopen the investigation into his brother's assassination. His own assassination brought that to an end and many people believe his killing was never fully explained. The youngest brother of the President, Ted Kennedy, also believed that the mob played a role in the assassination of President Kennedy, although he is said to have changed his mind about it during the last few years of his life.

This novel begins in late summer of 1974. It was an interesting time. President Kennedy had been assassinated 11 years earlier; Robert

Kennedy, his brother, had become a United States senator and was assassinated in 1968 after winning the California presidential primary; and the third brother, Ted Kennedy, had become a United States senator and during the 1970s was quietly making plans to run for the Office of President. If the Italian mob did play a part in killing President Kennedy, there would very likely be a few of its members who held that secret tightly while watching the third Kennedy brother prepare to run for the highest office in the land. There is no doubt they would have quietly rallied their forces to oppose him.

It is also interesting that during this period, the time during which this novel takes place, a well-documented three-sided war among Italians criminals, Irish criminals and union bosses was taking place in Cleveland, Ohio. It was a vicious conflict in which car bombings were an all too common weapon of choice that inflicted death and destruction on many innocent people.

In the previous Anthony Martino book, *Laugh at the Devil*, Judge Archer was revealed as a powerful and evil force whose influence extended beyond his home in Clinton County, Pennsylvania. This may seem unlikely to some readers. However, in Pennsylvania county and state judges often have enormous political power, and in some cases they use it for illegal purposes. In *Laugh at the Devil*, Judge Archer runs an operation that "sells" children from an orphanage to desperate couples who were unable to have children of their own. It should be noted that *Laugh at the Devil* was written prior to charges being filed against two anthracite region judges who inappropriately placed hundreds of juveniles into for-profit detention centers and benefited financially for doing so. The point is that *Laugh at the Devil* was not specifically "inspired" by the behavior of these judges. In a sense, it was "predictive" of behavior, which has been described as the worst judicial misconduct in the history of the United States! Moreover, within the last few years other Pennsylvania judges have been convicted of criminal activity while they were on the bench.

THE OAK TREE

Clinton County, Pennsylvania
Summer, 1974

Tears rolled down her cheeks as she read the headline: *Murdered: Judge and Priest.* Olga was more than the housekeeper and watched knowing Melissa would react with great emotion. They lived under the same roof and Olga loved and in her own way protected all of them: Melissa; her infant daughter; Tony Martino, Melissa's fiancée; and his two sons. Olga watched as Melissa continued to read and cry … when she began to shake … as she fell to her knees and buried her face in the paper.

Melissa knew he was a violent criminal, yet she loved him. He tricked her into having her daughter rather than an abortion, demonstrating his ability to manipulate her as well as his innate love of children and desire for a family. She loved him; she hated him; she knew of his many talents; and she recognized her inability to move beyond his reach, so she agreed to marry him. She wondered, however, if she could influence his behavior. *One way or another*, she thought, *I know he's involved in both killings, but I can't figure out how or why. He knew and loved the Monsignor since he was a child, and I can't imagine why he would have killed Judge Archer. His conflict with the Judge was behind him and Tony got everything he wanted. He even seduced the Judge's wife and broke up their marriage. He had no reason to kill someone who was defeated and humiliated, yet the police will consider Tony a prime suspect in the Judge's murder. Oh God, I hope he was careful. I don't want him to go to jail.*

Melissa looked at her shaking hands and tried to compose herself. Intellectually she was his equal although there were other dimensions to his personality that she could neither match nor understand. She continued to ponder. *The Judge was a respected public figure although he had many enemies, including Tony. Monsignor Lessari, on the other hand, had only one enemy that I'm aware of—Judge Archer. And since they were murdered on the same day, I'm certain their killings are connected.*

The newspaper was scattered about on the living room floor and Olga stood next to Melissa. "Where's Tony?" she asked Olga.

"Outside."

"Please watch the children," she said softly, although she knew it wasn't necessary to tell Olga.

He was standing with his back to her and the house. The magnificent white oak tree appeared to be the object of his attention and a soft wind seemed to speak as it moved over its branches and caused the leaves to move in unpredictable ways. She watched, hoping to learn the state of his mind, and noticed that the river sparkled in the valley below competing with the oak tree for his attention.

"Will the wind tell you who killed them, or do you know?"

A hawk flew over and for a brief time his eyes followed it. "The world is convulsing in a sea of inconsistencies and evil, while a bird of prey soars above all of it and patiently waits for an unsuspecting victim to reveal itself."

She tried again. "You think God speaks to you on the wind. It's nothing more than your imagination. It might even be the Devil or some other evil force. Your arrogance and twisted beliefs in God, the Devil and the afterlife distort your thinking."

"You hated both of them; you should be glad they're dead."

"They were murdered!"

His focus returned to the tree and the movement of air. The natural and spiritual worlds were part of a seamless universe he seemed to understand. He believed that God had spoken to him in the past and it was always on the wind. He also believed the Archangel Gabriel spoke to him the same way, on the wind. The Devil. He wasn't sure if the Prince of Darkness or any of his disciples had ever spoken to him, although he knew there was a vast reservoir of evil within his soul that would please the fallen angel. And Mary. He adored her and was convinced he had once killed on her behalf. The Archangel Gabriel, her sword, had conveyed The Holy Mother's wishes to him on the wind, or so he believed.

The deaths of two prominent people, both of whom he knew very well, would mean that law enforcement agencies would place him and other Italian American criminals under intense scrutiny. Yet he was confident he would survive although others might not. "This won't interfere with our wedding plans," he said, without looking at her.

She hesitated, angry that he was certain of her. At times, she wasn't sure she loved him and had told him so. She also said she wouldn't share her bed with him until she was ready. Yet he was sure she would marry him. Time and time again events that neither of them controlled thrust them into each other's lives. He would always be in her life, she reasoned. It seemed inevitable, so she said, "Yes." Their union would also mean that her infant daughter would have a father who loved her and would provide both of them with a lavish lifestyle. "All right, our wedding plans will go on as planned, but this better not become a problem." She held up the newspaper so the headline was visible.

A nod, without emotion, followed by an unusual burst of wind, ended their conversation. He continued to stare at the tree and listen to the sounds of the gentle movement of air, hoping to hear or feel something of value from the natural or spirit worlds; and to prepare himself for what would follow knowing the two killings would produce stress in the Clinton County courthouse—where Judge Archer had been a political boss whose influence extended well beyond the county. It would also produce deep anxiety within the criminal organizations that operated in and around the hard coal region of Pennsylvania.

Law enforcement agencies would examine the criminals who knew the two men and Tony Martino knew both of them better than anyone. They would take a long, hard look at him. Yet he looked forward to it because life without conflict and challenge had little value to him. But marrying Melissa and building a family mattered more than anything else, and he was well on his way to having both. Her infant daughter, Sarah, and his two sons, Michael and Timmy, were just the beginning. He wanted more children. He was determined to do it all: build a family, further his education and continue his life of crime. And when asked, he would serve God as only he could—by killing those who were evil. Life was a game, an exciting game for Tony Martino, one he played both brilliantly and alone—as a lone wolf, *Lupo Solitario.*

Weeks earlier, as Melissa planned for their wedding, he responded to her many questions about what their lives would be like. "The only certainty in life is uncertainty," he told her. Later that day he revealed more of himself when he added, "Laws and rules don't matter very much. Only family, friends and God are important." Underlying those cryptic statements were, however, layers of complex relationships with friends, family and other criminals.

Outwardly he looked calm, yet his guts were churning. His marriage to Melissa was of prime importance and he was confident they would marry, even though she had slipped away from him once. He would do everything possible to make sure it didn't happen again, even though he still found himself drawn to other women, including Melissa's sister Carol.

There were many chambers within Tony Martino's mind. Love for family and friends were near the place where his love for the Virgin Mary and respect for holy places and saintly individuals were stored. Yet deep canyons of uncertainty separated those areas of goodness from the dark enclaves where his evil deeds and ability to do harm were housed. At times, he moved with ease from the areas of goodness to those of darkness, especially when confronted by circumstances that would require his aptitudes for violence and manipulation that could stretch on for months. During those prolonged periods, he was consumed by a fear that he would be unable to return from the darkness. Yet at other times he considered allowing the evil that was within him to engulf and permanently take hold of all that he was. For it was his evil deeds that distinguished him from other men; that brought him great satisfaction and in a perverted way produced what he saw as justice where little of it had existed before. And so, these thoughts emerged: *It is God that allows evil to exist. Evil that I must turn my back to in cowardice or confront with cunning and violence. I choose the later, realizing that by killing those who embrace the Devil, I too become a demon the Devil would gladly welcome into Hell. Holy Mother, please remain with me if I once again descend into darkness.* Although he killed skillfully and with purpose, there was no joy in the abyss he feared and had entered with each killing, only darkness, hate and pain.

He decided to head north into the perimeter of thick undergrowth that bordered the area on top of the mountain around his home, knowing his son had left early in the morning and was probably somewhere in the forest. Then he entered the forest of towering old-growth trees that had survived the logging that raped most of the land of North Central Pennsylvania, as coal mining had done in the region of Pennsylvania where he was raised. Steep rugged approaches and the Dead Indian Swamp protected the forest, many acres of which he owned. He reasoned that God wasn't making any more forests or swamps, so he intended to buy more of the land adjoining the nearly two thousand acres he currently owned. Income from his legal and illegal enterprises would allow him to protect what he had and buy more.

There are more than 200 swamps in Pennsylvania, some of the largest of which are located on top of the long plateau-like mountains of the north-central area of the state. Many birds, rare flowers, quicksand and some of the world's largest black bears can be found in and around these areas. To some the swamps offer great beauty and biological diversity. To others they are places where danger and the smell of death are all too common. Yet men have for many years been drawn to swamps. Not surprisingly, in remote regions of Pennsylvania gravesites, including those of Native Americans, can be found hidden in and near the swamps.

Once he entered the forest he moved quickly, no longer hampered by the undergrowth. Although the day was clear and the sun was high in the sky, it was cool and the light was subdued, as if dawn were approaching; it was also quiet. Feeling the presence of someone or something he moved deliberately and controlled his breathing so as not to interfere with what he might hear. It was close … it was not a threat … he stopped and searched. He suddenly felt something else, or did he hear it, more than a hundred yards off near a steep drop off that he knew well. A great horned owl watched him move away. It would remain in its lofty perch until after the sun had left the sky. It killed its prey in darkness and rested during daylight near the ceiling of the forest canopy. It had been largely undetected for more than six years and had seen many things: children playing, young men and women making love, the burial of loved ones, and once it witnessed two men fighting and the victor hauling off the body of the other man for disposal in the swamp.

Tony took great care to move quietly. Though it too was silent, he was drawn to it and to the area. It was a special place where he recognized many of the rocks and trees. The spirits of many souls could very well be in the area; for their remains were left there by those who loved them and in some cases by those who hated and killed them. The forest, the swamp and the steep cliffs were believed by some to be holy land so they left their dead there. A man Tony murdered; his first wife; and his friend Tommy, the father of Melissa's daughter Sarah, were but a few of the departed who had been laid to rest in the area. And for hundreds of years the Indians buried their loved ones there. With concern in his heart he approached the area he was drawn to; the spot where he and his son Michael had released the ashes of Alysia, Michael's mother and his deceased wife. She had died just one year earlier and they still felt the pain of her passing. A dark form had its back to him. It was Michael. Alysia had been a good wife and suddenly Tony silently wept for her. "I know you're here," Michael said, without turning or looking up.

"What are you doing here?" She had been cremated and the father and son had released her ashes just a short distance away, so Tony spoke softly.

He still hadn't looked in the direction of his father. "I like it here, but someone was into my mother's things." He pointed in the direction of a small mound of rocks. After Tony and Michael released her ashes they buried her cremation urn and marked the spot with the mound. If Michael was correct ... Tony became angry, although he didn't show his emotions.

Michael was only 13 years old, but he was half Indian and had a deep understanding of the forest, wild animals and the wind that so frequently captured Tony's attention. He also had incredible visual and hearing acuity. "How did you know I was in the forest?" Tony asked, testing Michael's abilities.

"I heard you before you stopped near the owl," Michael replied. He then slowly moved his left hand back and forth over the area he was examining.

Tony had felt the presence of the owl although he never saw it. "Everything looks right to me. Why do you think someone dug up your mother's urn?"

"The rocks aren't the way we left them ... You know the coin you put in the urn?"

"What about it?"

"Was it gold?"

"Yeah."

"I'll bet it's gone."

While he was in Arizona, Tony killed the man who had the gold and made it look like suicide. At gun point he forced the man, who was once married to Michael's mother, to drink Tequila until he was numbingly drunk. Then he offered to spare his life if he told Tony where his fortune in gold coins was hidden. After telling Tony the location, he passed out after a few more glasses of Tequila. Tony started the car in the enclosed garage next to the office where the victim was sprawled on the floor. Exhaust fumes quickly filled the garage and house. Tony carried away the gold and left behind no physical evidence that he had been there. Although the local police had their doubts, the coroner ruled the victim had committed suicide. Months later, after Tony had returned to Pennsylvania, he converted some of the gold into cash. One gold coin, however, was placed by Tony into Alysia's cremation urn before it was buried. The gold coins were never important to Tony, but they were to her. He believed it was fitting to bury one inside her urn, below the mound that he and Michael had built at the spot where her ashes had been released.

Tony began to carefully remove rocks from the mound. Once they were arranged off to his right side, he dug with his hands through the soft sandy earth until the urn was reached. "Son-of-a-bitch," he said with a soft growl. The urn was empty.

Also composed, also furious, Michael said, "Kill whoever did it!"

Anger and concern about Michael's reaction found their way into Tony's thinking. *The police must be looking around to see if they can find something to nail me with. One of them stole the gold coin. Oh God, Michael's talking about killing someone! ... I figured they'd be looking at me real close, but if they didn't have a search warrant they trespassed on my property. I should get my lawyer involved ... Huh, Michael is a bright kid, figuring this out. But killing ... I don't want him to follow me into Hell. And yet he could help me. And besides, he's a smart, tough kid with a strong sense of himself. He's my son and although I didn't father him, he's like me. I can guide him; show him the choices that life offers and help him become whatever it is that comes naturally to him ... Oh God, I hope it isn't killing.*

Michael fixed his dark eyes on Tony. "What should we do?"

"We'll stay off all trails, even those made by animals, and travel north, paralleling the path that was probably taken by the bastards who did this. Then we'll cut back to the path and follow it back here. Unless they were very careful, we should be able to find some clues."

They stayed on the swamp side of the path and moved carefully, avoiding areas where the swamp seemed to move under their feet, an indication that deadly quicksand might be nearby. When they arrived at a Y in the path, after walking for nearly an hour, Tony explained, "Whoever it was that trespassed on our land, he or they came in on one of these two paths, so this is a good place to start and work our way back to the spot where your mother's urn is buried." Knowing they could easily identify their starting point, Tony walked on the riverside of the path and Michael on the swamp side.

The path was rarely used and branches and vines obstructed their movement. Tony was looking down at the path and the area on both sides, while he gently moved vegetation that obstructed his passage. "Daddy, look!" his son said, as he pointed to the freshly broken branch of a maple tree. It was shoulder high and someone broke it easily, without thinking, as they moved it out of their way while walking the path. The inner bark was green and the wood was light brown and hadn't yet dried out. It was all the physical evidence Tony needed. An animal couldn't have broken the small branch. It was too high. An intruder had recently, within the previous two days, walked along the path.

The wrapper from a piece of hard candy was found a short time later. Never touched, it was left in place and a mental note was made of its location. They had nearly reached the spot where the urn was buried when Michael stopped his father and pointed toward the swamp. There it was in the soft damp ground: two sets of footprints off the path and then back. They had relieved themselves and left behind irrefutable evidence that they had been there, near the spot where Tony and Michael had buried a gold coin in the cremation urn.

As they walked back to their home, Michael again asked, "What are you going to do?" Tony was deep in thought and didn't respond.

"Two cops trespassed on my property and stole a gold coin from the site my son and I built to honor my deceased wife," Tony told Sheriff Marsit over the telephone. "Get over here and take a look."

The Sheriff was a trusted friend although this wasn't the first time he needed to keep friendship and his role as a police officer separated from each other. When dealing with Tony it was especially difficult, because their friendship ran deep and Tony had once helped him deal with a legal problem that could have ended his career in law enforcement.

The Sheriff took careful notes while he talked to Michael and Tony on the porch of their home. Melissa held Sarah and silently listened. She was concerned when she realized that Michael was angry beyond anything she had ever seen in a young boy. Her concern grew when the Sheriff asked, "Tony, you said there were two sets of footprints, but how do you know they're police officers?"

"Because it happened within the last two days, and we both know state cops are asking a lot of questions about me and my family … aren't they?"

"That's pretty thin."

"Did they have a search warrant, Carl?" Tony stared at his friend.

"I don't know anything about search warrants."

"It doesn't matter." Melissa insisted. "With or without a search warrant, the police do not have the right to steal anything, especially from a place Michael and Tony set aside to honor Michael's mother. And Tony is right. Only the police would come that far onto our property, remove a gold coin, rebuild the mound of stones and leave. That mound was untouched for nearly a year. You're a fool or a dishonest cop yourself if you don't see the connection between the police investigating the two murders and the missing gold coin!"

The discussion continued for a short time before Vito Martin, Tony's attorney, arrived and became involved in the discussion. The three men: Sheriff Carl Marsit, Vito and Tony were friends who hunted, gambled and played basketball together. But this was serious business that Vito believed could give Tony an excuse to behave rashly. He told Tony and Melissa, "If a state police officer wanted to enter your property for surveillance purposes, he could do it legally without Carl knowing anything about it. He would first need to convince the county district attorney, and with that endorsement he would seek approval from a judge and probably get it."

"The district attorney was friends with Judge Archer." Tony answered. "He's part of the courthouse gang the Judge controlled up to the time he was killed."

"Yes, but before you jump to any conclusions, Tony, remember that you're not certain it was a police officer. And I'll tell you something that Carl won't appreciate. Some police officers play fast and loose with the rules, especially state police. I wouldn't be surprised if one or more of them entered your property without a search warrant, hoping to get something they could use against you."

Carl remained silent because he had more than once done exactly that, ignored the rules. Ironically, Vito and Tony helped him when he could have landed in jail for beating the hell out of a drunk teenage driver.

Melissa had become more worldly since she graduated from college. "I can understand a cop entering our property to see if Tony is doing something illegal. I don't like it, but I can understand it. But if a cop steals something, I won't have any sympathy for him if Tony beats the hell out of him!"

The three men retraced the path Tony and his son took earlier in the day. Photographs and measurements were taken of the footprints, and the candy wrapper was carefully placed into a plastic bag. Tony hoped a fingerprint could be found on the wrapper. The Sheriff didn't think it was possible. He did, however, recognize the candy wrapper although he didn't say anything to Tony. A state cop who was assigned to the area before joining the Pennsylvania Crime Commission often ate the same candy.

THE BIG PICTURE

Luzerne County, Pennsylvania

hree times the Monsignor had blessed his knife, and three times Tony had murdered with it. He slowly rotated the knife on the long table while the other five men watched without saying anything. Knowing they were watching gave Tony a sense of pride. He wondered how many of them knew he had used it to kill the Monsignor less than one week earlier. Joey, his cousin, knew but could never tell anyone. How could he? It was his killing of Judge Archer that drove Tony to kill the Monsignor. The Monsignor had entered Tony's world and lied to him about the most serious of issues—a killing. Tony had no choice but to kill him, as he would have killed anyone but a blood relative, before he became a powerful untrustworthy force within the mob. The Monsignor had agreed that it was up to Tony to decide if the Judge would be murdered. But once he realized that Tony wouldn't do it, the Monsignor back-doored him by directing his cousin Joey to kill the Judge. Incredibly, when Tony killed the Monsignor for ordering the Judge's murder, he believed God expected him to kill the Priest he had known since he was a child.

The three Martinos sat quietly on one side of a long table facing three equally grim Capilanos. As was his practice, Tony Martino physically separated himself as much as possible from everyone, even the other Martinos, while he continued rotating the knife with his right hand. Jake Capilano knew Tony took great pride in the knife. He knew that he had ended the lives of at least two men with it. It was his guess that Tony had also used it to murder Monsignor Lessari although he couldn't come up with any reason for him killing the Priest that he had loved and respected since his childhood. The silence had lasted for more than twenty minutes before Jake said, "Frank, how long do you think this will take?"

Frank answered with a shrug and continued to stare at Jake with a blank look on his face. Frank was the undisputed head of the Martino family and would receive complete support from Tony, his son, and Joey, his nephew. The three Martinos: Frank, Tony and Joey, were skilled killers who had each taken the lives of more men and with greater skill than any Capilano. If a conflict erupted in the room before or during the meeting, Jake knew that he and his nephews, Danny and Jack, would die. If they were lucky they might kill one of the Martinos.

The murders of Judge Archer in Clinton County, and Monsignor Lessari in Luzerne County, took place on the same day and shocked the people of the area. Pennsylvania law enforcement agencies immediately launched aggressive investigations. It was widely known that the Monsignor was a friend of many Italian criminals in hard coal country, and that Tony Martino and Judge Archer were bitter enemies. Tony and his family found themselves at the center of the investigation that quickly spread to the rest of the hard coal region's criminal organization, including legal and illegal enterprises controlled by the Capilanos.

Law enforcement personnel were certain Tony was the key to solving the crimes although there was no evidence to link him to either killing. The Capilanos were also sure and were furious that they were suddenly under intense scrutiny because of two murders they had no part in. Yet the past was dead and Jake Capilano, the head of his family and overall boss of the region's mob, wanted it to stay that way. However, Jake's control over the mob was at best tenuous.

Two years earlier Jake's brother, Mario Capilano, planned to kill Enrico Scarpati as part of a bold plan to break free from the New York City family that controlled much of Pennsylvania and exerted considerable influence over the areas it didn't completely dominate. Because they were related by blood, the Martino family came to Enrico's defense and in less than six hours had killed the three best Capilano soldiers and placed Mario into a position where only his death could prevent the killing of more Capilanos, including his son Jack. The conflict ended the only way it could, with Mario Capilano's death. Mario put a bullet in his head.

Jake remembered it very clearly including the irony of it all. Mario's attempt to increase the power of the Capilano crime family instead transformed the tough but honest Martino family into a violent and tight knit group based on blood loyalties, within the larger criminal organization. In some ways, the part that was created so quickly in the midst of bloodshed, was greater than the whole.

Rocco Capilano was probably the first one killed by the Martinos. His skull was crushed by someone with enormous strength who enjoyed the feel and smell of his victim. Knowing he was the one, Neil glanced at Joey for a moment and thought it strange that he was nervous. "Joey fears no one but God and Monsignor Lessari," was a refrain the Martinos and Joey's friends often repeated.

Frankie Cannon was killed with a knife while working in his office. His killer then planted an ice pick directly above his penis. Killing with a knife and a sick joke meant Tony did it. Jake was certain of it. Still deep inside himself, Tony now repeatedly moved a small stone slowly down the full length of his knife while Jake took a long look at him. Tony was usually smiling and talkative, but not since the day of the two killings.

Angelo Capilano was the third Capilano soldier murdered in the first few hours of their conflict with the Martinos. A single bullet to the head from close range didn't tell Jake much about the person who pulled the trigger, and that bothered him. He knew Joey, Frank and Tony were skilled killers but had no idea how many other Martinos had committed murder and would answer violence with far greater violence if the current tension between the two families erupted into a second war.

"Goddamn it," Danny Capilano suddenly screamed at Tony. "You probably killed Monsignor Lessari with that fucking knife!"

Tony immediately jumped to his feet. Leaving little doubt as to his intentions, he held the knife firmly; low and slightly behind him, the ideal position for a quick, powerful thrust forward. Time moved slowly during the drama ... a step forward, the knife drawn back further ... Danny leaned back and turned away ... Frank and Joey stood with their guns drawn ... Jake unexpectedly struck Danny with the back of his right fist, then with a left hook to his face. Leaving no room for misunderstanding his intentions and loyalties, Jack delivered a clenched right fist to the back of the head. The five men return to their earlier positions. The room was again silent. Danny remained on the floor, unconscious and bleeding. Jake and Jack saved Danny's life and delivered a clear message—the Capilanos did not want another war with the Martinos.

Time passed. Danny regained consciousness and thought about what had happened to him and what it would mean to his girlfriend Carol, who was standing just outside the door. He quietly returned to his chair pausing only to wipe blood from his face. Then there was a soft knock on the door. "Enter!" Tony shouted.

"Mr. DeGalanti is parking his car, Tony," Carol said nervously. She glanced quickly around the room before closing the door behind her. She noticed the blood on her boyfriend's face and didn't react.

As Carol continued to play *sentinel* at the office door, the intensity of her thoughts increased. Her personal sense of importance could not be denied. Only she knew how she felt standing there *on guard*, so to speak, and she inwardly smirked at her new-found status and reflected on what led her to this moment. She often re-evaluated her situation with Tony and always reached the same conclusion. Had she compromised herself? *Yes!* Had she deceived her sister to get to this point in time? *Yes!* But she was always quick to justify her actions in the recesses of her mind. The smugness continued as she analyzed internally. Although she had a boyfriend, she was still Tony's whore and she loved it. He was going to marry Melissa, but when she and Tony were together he did things with her, she was certain, he didn't do with her sister. Things men don't do with their wives. She smiled inwardly, still standing at the door, and a surge of power almost exploded inside her. Yet she needed to keep her sense of euphoria secret.

Her boyfriend was only a minor distraction for Carol, even knowing he was behind the door sitting not far from Tony. In the scheme of things, she reasoned, she was an integral part of Tony's enterprise; a part of his life that was secret from many people who thought they knew him well. After all, she was on guard duty with instructions from Tony Martino. She was on the outside of a secret room where a most secret meeting was taking place. The powerful, violent men participating would not hesitate to kill anyone who violated any part of their code, and that included her.

Then another thought raced through her head, quickly changing her mood. Perhaps she loved as well as lusted for Tony. She suddenly became pensive as the thought of her boyfriend again crossed her mind. He could present a significant problem for her. Men like Tony don't take lightly to liaisons with the enemy. Her boyfriend was a member of the Capilano family and she was well aware of what had happened during the Martino-Capilano War. But she would worry about that later. This was here and now, and as quickly as the dark thoughts came they vanished. Suddenly she became alert. "Yes, Carol would be just fine," she said to herself. She knew the cards she had been dealt, how to play the hand, and she had no intention of folding.

Frank and Jake knew Neil DeGalanti would run the meeting. He would seek answers and make suggestions. If things didn't turn out to his liking he would raise his voice and tell people what to do. Then, if necessary, he would become sinister, soft spoken and make threats that had meaning. Nevertheless, Frank and Jake knew the drill and had survived in the past when other men died. World War Two and the Martino-Capilano War had hardened them.

The door swung open and Neil held it for a small, thin, well-dressed man in his early sixties. Although they had never before come face-to-face with him, Frank and Jake recognized him and immediately stood. Neil's father, Cosmo DeGalanti, was the head of the New York City family that controlled the hard coal region's criminal organization for more than 40 years. He had barely entered the room when Jake took his hand and said, "It's an honor to meet you." They kissed each other on both cheeks as the older DeGalanti scanned the room, stopping when he saw Danny's swollen face. His attention jumped to the rear corner of the room. "For Christ's sake, Tony," he shouted. "I told you, *remember the big picture,* and you do this!"

Jake was caught off-guard, as were the others, not knowing how or why the head of the family knew Tony. "Tony didn't do it," Jake answered apologetically. "Danny was out of line, so I taught him a lesson."

Frank Martino extended his right hand. "I've heard many fine things about you. Your words regarding our current problems will serve us well." After shaking hands, Frank regained his composure and embraced Cosmo DeGalanti. They kissed on both cheeks.

Cosmo didn't greet or acknowledge the other men in the room, turning instead to his son he said, "Neil, you sit here and run the meeting. I'll sit back with that hot head," as he glared at Tony.

Neil did as his father instructed knowing he wouldn't tolerate insubordination, not even from his son. Yet it was clear Neil was surprised by his father's words and behavior. *How does my father know Tony,* he thought? *I never told him who took care of business for me in Pennsylvania and he didn't seem to care. He listened when I told others that Lupo Solitario was the muscle, the enforcer who protected our interests in Central and Northeast Pennsylvania. Everyone, including my father, quickly realized that a "lone wolf" killer needed to remain anonymous. How and when did he and Tony come to know each other? Yeah, and why would he want to know Tony?*

The meeting commenced. Frank and then Joey sat directly to Neil's left. Proximity to Neil signified status in the family, so to Neil's right Jake, Jack and then Danny sat in that order. Unconcerned about status, Tony wanted to physically distance himself from the others. He positioned himself at the far end of the long table. The older DeGalanti and Tony had greeted each other with a hug and kisses on both cheeks before Cosmo sat off to Tony's side. He was the five hundred-pound gorilla in the room that tried to sit unnoticed while the others dealt with a problem that should have been of little consequence to a man who controlled the second largest crime family in New York City, and nearly two hundred other criminals spread across New Jersey, the Philadelphia area and the hard coal region of Pennsylvania.

Frank and Jake told Neil the little they knew about the killings of the Judge and Monsignor while the others remained silent. "Anything you want to add?" Neil asked Joey.

Tony had returned to slowly rotating his knife on the table with his index finger, but he stopped when Joey answered, "Me? I'm like Uncle Frank and Jake. I only know what's in the newspapers. There's lots of talk on the streets, but nothing that makes sense."

They had been friends for more than five years. Neil knew Tony was brilliant, violent and capable of killing with both stealth and pride. He had killed at Neil's request; he had killed to protect his family and their business interests; and Neil suspected that he had at times murdered when a blind rage took hold of his soul. Tony would never admit to anyone that he had committed murder. Even when done at his request, Tony was reluctant to discuss the specifics of a murder with Neil for fear that his words would one day be used against him. Brilliant, secretive and violent; Tony Martino was a powerful force in the anthracite region's criminal world. Yet until this point he had said nothing at the meeting. "What about you, Tony?" Jake asked. "Or are you dumb and blind?"

Neil waited for an answer as he noticed his father, who was sitting next to Tony, was staring at him with a strange look on his face. "The Monsignor probably had the Judge killed and then someone killed the Monsignor to settle the score," Tony replied with a flat voice; without emotion.

Cosmo DeGalanti's expression didn't change and the other men in the room were only slightly surprised by Tony's response. Jake spoke for them in a firm voice when he said, "Ya got anything to back that up Tony; or are you just pulling it out of your ass?"

"Go fuck yourself, asshole!"

"Tony!" his father shouted, "Show some respect! And Jake, for Christ's sake, we're looking for ideas, and it ain't a bad one."

"I agree, it's a good idea," Jack Capilano said. Jack had been his friend since ninth grade and Tony twice saved his life. Yet he knew very little of the conflict between Tony and Judge Archer over Tony's efforts to adopt Timmy. He only knew the Judge blocked the adoption until he received a payoff and that Tony had been furious about it.

Tony was willing to accept a system of government based on bribes and illegal favors, but not when it came to the welfare of children. The intense and at times public conflict between Judge Archer and Tony was watched by many people in Clinton County and hard coal country. Yet they didn't know the reason for the conflict. Even before Tony seduced the Judge's wife and publicly displayed his relationship with her, they hated each other. When Jack heard the Judge was murdered he incorrectly assumed that Tony was responsible. He also assumed that Tony had planned it down to the last detail, as he had seen him do in the past when killing was involved. Still, the murders of the Judge and the Monsignor on the same day were inconsistent with a well laid plan unless … Jack silently searched for answers. *I'll bet one of Judge Archer's friends killed Monsignor Lessari after Tony killed the Judge. They did it for revenge or because they thought the Monsignor played a hand in the Judge's murder. That's how it must have played out. Oh God, this isn't over. Tony will get even!*

Neil also knew of the conflict between Tony and Judge Archer, and the close relationship Tony had with the Monsignor. "We ain't the police or the FBI, so the truth isn't necessary, only the perceptions of *our truth* are needed. Can we create the idea that the killings are connected the way Tony said, and sell it to people we depend on; maybe even the cops?"

Jack again answered, "The Judge and Monsignor had a fist fight at Tony's home that was witnessed by a lot of people, including a cop. The Monsignor kicked his ass! I agree we don't need to establish an accurate story of what happened. Hell, we don't even know what really happened. Rumors and perceptions are good enough, with a few facts to back it up."

"A good lie is better than a set of facts that can harm our interest," the older DeGalanti added, while continuing to stare at his son.

Neil knew what his father wanted and for the first time he began to understand why his father left the city to deal with an issue that still seemed to him of little importance. He was there to support Tony, to make things go his way. Neil again wondered why, even as he said, "We all know Tony is a master of the big con; manipulating people, even the police, into doing what he wants them to do." Neil cringed at his own words because he knew Tony had somehow staged what was about to follow. "Tony, it's your idea, so do whatever it takes. And be careful, damn it. None of this bull in a china shop crap. Jake and your father will help you if it's needed, and they'll keep me informed."

Tony smiled and Neil noted that his father gave him a gentle nudge with his elbow, signifying his approval of what had just happened. Thinking the meeting was over, Neil stood, followed by Jake and Frank. However, Cosmo DeGalanti said, "Please sit, there is something I wish to share with you." He stood very slowly adding importance to the words he was about to speak. "The strength and greatness of Rome often depended on its provinces. This, as well as lessons from recent history, should be our guide as we prepare for what I believe will be a threat to our enterprises and friends over the next few years." Cosmo DeGalanti was a self-educated man and often inserted historical references into his discussions with family and criminal associates. Feared for his cunning and brutality, he was also respected for his wisdom and was called *The Historian* by many who knew him. Yet Neil was suddenly embarrassed because he knew of absolutely nothing that could threaten the New York City crime families. If a threat did emerge, he couldn't see how the Italian criminals of the anthracite region could possibly help the five powerful crime families whose operations extended to Italy, Latin America, Canada and several other areas of the United States. Nevertheless, not wanting to show his ignorance, Jake said, "Would you like to give the group a general idea about what they should expect?"

"A general idea ... Yes, I can do that. First, I want everyone to hear directly from me why I am here today. A conflict between the

Martino and Capilano families would create an opportunity for our common enemy to move in and establish relationships with police, elected officials and our church. Therefore, I shall not tolerate the killing of anyone from either family unless Frank Martino and Jake Capilano both agree that it is necessary—Capeesh?"

"I understand and agree fully," Jake replied. Frank Martino wasn't as enthusiastic although he added, "Same here."

"With all due respect Mister DeGalanti, who is the enemy?" Jack asked.

"The Irish," he replied with fire in his voice, as he struck the table with his right fist. "With our help, an Irish American became the only Roman Catholic ever elected president. He and his family begged us for help with unions and money; and they asked for help rigging the vote, especially in Chicago. Without our help in Pennsylvania, West Virginia and Illinois, he would never have been elected. And how did he and his family repay us? Once he became president, that whore mongering Irish bastard used his brother to come after us. But the two of them made many enemies and they died the way evil men should." He paused and took a slow drink from a glass of water while his son became nervous, as he had in the past whenever his father celebrated the assassinations of the Irish-American President and his brother. Then Cosmo DeGalanti added, "They died covered in their own blood, murdered by men of low quality."

"Father," Neil said, "why bring up the past? They got what they deserved, so it's over."

Neil had spoken softly and with respect, but it didn't matter. Anger was on his father's face and his words were filled with venom. "The Irish family that cheated us in the past will try once again to elevate one of their men to the nation's highest office." He paused, then added, "This time we will oppose them every step of the way!"

Frank respected the head of the criminal organization he was part of, an association he could never have imagined only five years earlier. During the Battle of the Bulge, however, he learned that men in positions of authority were far from infallible and were capable of giving orders that could have disastrous consequences for those below them. He spoke up. "Interfering in a presidential election would be a high stakes gamble for us and we could come out on the short end no matter who wins. If we remain neutral things will remain the way they are; and things ARE good."

Long before he became part of the mob, Frank Martino was widely known and respected throughout the hard coal region, especially in the Italian-American community. A man who had been a coal miner, union official, bartender, baker and a World War Two hero had paid his dues. That, coupled with his leadership of the Martino family during their war with the Capilanos, made him a man Cosmo DeGalanti could not easily dismiss. Neil had told him how Frank and the other Martinos protected Enrico Scarpati, the DeGalanti appointed head of the anthracite region's Italian criminals, during the war between the two families. Because Frank Martino deserved respect, Cosmo DeGalanti selected his words carefully. "The leading members of the New England Irish political machine believe that we played a role in killing the President and his brother, the Senator. Publicly they are careful to accept the conclusions of the federal investigations which indicated that lone gunmen were the assassins. However, all my sources tell me they privately believe the Italian mob, as they call us, was responsible for both killings. If their candidate, the youngest brother of the President, is elected, he will focus all available law enforcement on us. We cannot allow that to happen, so we must prevent him from becoming president."

His words resulted in deep silence. Even Neil was stunned at his father's reference to the two assassinations. He recalled how his father, who normally showed little emotion, jumped to his feet laughing when he first heard of the assassination of the President, and with a smile told him, "The hand of justice can strike down even a powerful man when he arrogantly turns against those who helped him achieve greatness." Six years later, when the President's brother also died from an assassin's bullet, he again found reasons to be overjoyed. "The Irish bastards who responded to our cooperation with contempt have received what every dishonorable man deserves—a brutal ending covered in his own blood!" And although he never said it, Neil often wondered if his father didn't know far more than he should have about the two assassinations. That fear was tempered, however, by the significant number of Italian criminals who openly claimed to be involved in the assassination of the President. Many Italian mob figures, some of whom were of high rank and others who were in prison with little hope of ever being released, boasted about playing a part in the President's death. They were ignored by law enforcement officials who grudgingly accepted the conclusions of the commissions specifically established to investigate the assassination.

Neil's father had a violent past including the murder of his own brother. It happened before Neil was born when control of the family was at stake. After his brother was eliminated, Cosmo became the uncontested head of the family. That killing, like so many things he did, was shrouded in layers of secrecy and uncertainty making it impossible for charges to be brought against him. Nobody, not even his son, was fully aware of his past criminal activities or what he had in mind for the future. Secretive, violent and brilliant; in many ways Cosmo DeGalanti and Tony Martino were alike.

The nervous quiet that had filled the room ended when Jake spoke. "I know the dead President's brother is the only Irish politician who has a chance of becoming president. But he's a drunken, womanizing, low-life who got away with raping a young girl. The only reason that coward isn't in jail right now is because his family has all the judges in their back pocket. Besides, he's not as smart as his two murdered brothers. Even with all his family's money backing him, he got thrown out of college for cheating on an exam. He won't even have a chance right here in Pennsylvania. The Protestant vote will go against him, and the Catholics will turn against him because of his cheating, drinking and whoring around. Hell, the dirt that's come out about his two dead brothers will haunt him."

Tony had tried not to become involved in the discussion thinking he had more immediate issues to deal with. Nevertheless, he replied, "The Church will support him behind the scenes, so Catholics will probably vote for him."

"Now how in the hell could you possibly know that?" Jake asked mockingly.

"About a week before Monsignor Lessari was murdered, he told me that the Church was flooding Pennsylvania with as many Irish priests as possible and sending Italian priests off into areas where there were few Italian Americans. He knew the Vatican's representative to the United Nations; that's who told him. Money talks, especially with the hierarchy of the Catholic Church. He said the bishops and cardinals in the northeastern part of the country want to see another Catholic as president, and the only high profile Catholic politician is the dead President's brother. So, the Church worked out a strategy with his family that helps both sides. Money was and probably still is being funneled from his family into the right places within the Church in exchange for its support. We all know the Church can be bought, if you have enough money. You've done it, Jake." Jake cringed because Tony was referring to the death of his son-in-law. With Tony's help, he was murdered and it was made to look like a suicide. Because he was believed to have taken his own life, the Church initially refused to bury him. That changed quickly when Jake bribed the pastor of the Church for the sake of his daughter. Tony continued, "So our church is assigning Irish priests into areas where it will do the most good for Irish politicians."

"Why didn't you tell me immediately?" Cosmo DeGalanti shouted at Tony.

The discussion was moving into areas Tony was reluctant to talk about candidly, in spite of the common bonds that united the men in the room. "Look Mr. DeGalanti, until a few minutes ago I didn't know another Irish president would be a threat to our interests; you never told me."

He glared at Tony for what seemed like a long time, though it was only a few seconds. Then he replied, "You are right, Tony. I should have told you. There is much I will one day tell you and my son." He looked at Neil and continued. "Like all of you, I am uncomfortable becoming involved in national politics. It was always enough for us to have friends in the cities and states where we do business. In 1960 the Irish brought us into national politics and we were honored by their request for help. We were happy to set aside our past differences with the Irish so a greater good could be served; electing the first Roman

Catholic president in the history of our great nation. We helped them, he was elected, and then he and his brother stabbed us in the back! This will not happen again. The Irish hold many positions of power in government and within the Roman Catholic Church of this country. As long as Italians are dominant in crime and in the Vatican, we will accept that. But unions, gambling, the waterfronts of major ports, the police and courts in our areas; these are ours along with our other businesses. What is ours is ours, and we will fight to hold on to what we have. We will not stand by and allow them to acquire the presidency and once again cheat us. And you can be sure that if they eliminated us, they'd quickly move Irish criminals into our territories and into our businesses. We allowed the Westies, the Irish who feed off the crumbs we leave, to exist in New York City, our City. The Boston Irish politicians would quickly bring the criminal elements they work with in their area into a union with the Westies and attempt to destroy us. They will try to take the moral high ground in the back rooms where they are skilled at dealing with judges and priests. But they are no better than us. No, they are far worse!"

By the time the meeting ended, Jake and Frank agreed that an Irish American president who believed the Italian mob was involved in the killing of his brother, would be a far greater threat to their interests than the Capilanos and Martinos were to each other. Also, both men were deeply troubled by the likelihood that their church, the Roman Catholic Church, would actively work behind the scenes to help the Irish against them.

They knew that Tony, who once staunchly supported the Roman Catholic Church while ignoring many of its teachings, had expressed outright disdain for it since Monsignor Lessari had been murdered. Neither of them knew how or why he changed his mind, although it was obvious to both of them that he had. It seemed that circumstances surrounding the murder of the Monsignor had turned Tony against his religion. He continued to believe in God, adore Mary and would raise his children as Catholics; yet he now had nothing but contempt for his Church.

Neil DeGalanti left the meeting with serious concerns. Had his father established a relationship with Tony that could end with the death of the third brother from the President's family? And could the Church's evolving position against the Italians in favor of the Irish have led to the Monsignor's death—for he would have surely defied his church and worked in support of the Italians?

Carol heard the sound of heavy chairs moving away from a table and knew the meeting was over. She assumed her position, and then opened the door. Her boyfriend said nothing to her and had a strange look on his face as he left the room. She assumed he now hated her for whatever had happened to him inside, believing only the Martinos could have attacked him while he was behind the door she had guarded. She was happy for that, because of what she knew was about to happen.

Except for Tony, all of them left. He waited briefly before saying, "Come in here, Carol." She locked the door behind her. Melissa told her she hadn't made love to Tony in more than a year, so Carol knew he would be wild with desire. She decided it was inevitable and softly said, "Please God, forgive me."

He stood and faced her, pausing for a moment before telling her, "Take off your clothes."

POWER OF THE PRESS

A giant of a man, Big George was also a smart businessman who was willing to take reasonable risks in business and in life. When he couldn't find a decent job, he started a merchandising magazine with a small loan from his father. Distributed widely to numerous businesses, its only source of income was from advertising. Because of its many public service announcements; humorous and local interest pieces written by George; and an opinion section where people were permitted to comment on a wide range of issues, the magazine quickly became popular. After a few months, it also became highly profitable.

Not long after the magazine became a financial success, George bought a bar that he named Diamond Lil's. He advertised, *Good Food and Cheap Booze*, in his magazine and the local newspaper. But it was the edgy events and décor that brought in many customers, especially students and employees of the University. City officials and some business people cringed when *Favorite Erotic Masterpiece Night* was announced by George. The University's faculty and students, however, eagerly awaited the event hoping that it would become a cause célèbre. And George didn't disappoint them. Copies of paintings and photographs of nude females and males were on display and patrons crowded in nightly to see the naughty works.

George and Tony Martino became friends shortly after Tony arrived in Lock Haven as a student. Their bond grew stronger as

Tony supplied George with hot merchandise, especially high-quality liquor that helped make Diamond Lil's a financial success. Although they were both aggressive and enjoyed challenging the establishment, George was shocked when Tony approached him with an idea for a new business venture. "Are you out of your fucking mind, Martino? Turn my magazine into a goddamn newspaper!"

"This will work. I'll make it work."

"And your role?"

"I'll be out of sight, but I'll supply information, suggestions and money—the good kind, under the table money that's off the books. I'll also get some of my friends to feed you stuff about politicians—all off the record."

There were risks for George, though none were serious or unmanageable. He knew what Tony wanted; a powerful public voice that he could influence. "If I agree, what's the next step?"

Tony smiled and extended his right hand. Their grips were powerful and they held tightly when Tony answered, "Just start thinking about how you can convert your merchandiser into a news publication. You're smart, you'll figure it out."

A slight nod of approval, a tighter grip, followed by, "And the money?"

Convinced they had a deal Tony replied, "Melissa's sister Carol will be your accountant. She'll help with sales and distribution and she'll be the contact for the money you'll need." This wasn't the only role Tony had in mind for Carol, but it was an important one and would keep her close to him.

Money, a new business venture and a beautiful woman—George was hooked as he thought of the many possibilities. He suspected that Carol was involved with Tony, but that didn't bother him because he and Tony had done many things far worse than sharing a woman. Yet aside from her good looks and connections to Tony, he knew little about her.

That evening, after a long telephone conversation with Carol, George wrote the first of what would be hundreds of articles that would find their way into the still unnamed newspaper.

Dear Reader, I thought you should know

Each of us is the sum total of all our experiences combined with the physical and mental abilities given to us at birth. Such an obvious concept, yet it is frequently lost in the endless series of events, both important and trivial, which make up the days, weeks and years of our lives.

Opinions expressed by politicians, clergy, those who teach and those who write are important, as are their presentation of the facts, as well as the information they intentionally ignore. As a bartender, I gave little thought to the words I forcefully spoke knowing few people took me seriously. But now, as I write the first of what will become a series of articles, I feel compelled to honestly describe myself including the beliefs that are central to my very being.

Religion, or the search for God, is the single most important factor in the history of the human race. Like most people, I believe in God although like many of them I have grave reservations about religion—all religions. The more highly organized a religion is, the less I like it. Highly structured organizations devote too much time creating and enforcing rules that benefit themselves at the expense of the common good. That's a term, the common good, that religions and governments throughout the world rarely utter, for it's clear that both focus instead upon their own selfish needs and desires.

Government, like religion, is a necessary evil which is better when there is as little of it as possible. Furthermore, most of the great tragedies in human history occurred and continue to occur when religion and government come together to ruthlessly pursue the interests of one or both. The Cold War, with godless communists on one side and largely Christian democracies on the other, is rarely described that way. Perhaps it should be, although I recognize that other factors are involved in the struggle.

Government and religion define nations and determine the course of human history. In contrast, today more than ever it's education that largely defines the individual. Education received formally, informally and even accidentally determines *not just how we make a living. It has a major impact on how others view us; who we marry and associate with; whether or not we serve in the military and even where we live.*

I ended up in Lock Haven, Pennsylvania because my father was a professor and took a job there with the University. After I graduated from high school, my father told me to continue my education citing the obvious: I could walk to class, I didn't have any plans for my life, and because he worked for the University my tuition would be very low. After four years in the Army, two of which I spent in Vietnam, I realized my father was right. I returned to Pennsylvania and got a university degree. Then, with a little financial help from my father, I started a merchandising magazine and a few years later bought a bar and grill. And now I plan to write a series of articles in which I will describe the world as I see it.

You have been warned and informed! You know who I am, what I am and some of what I believe. With this in mind, please read what I write in the future.

The newspaper didn't have a name, but George's byline did— *Consider This.*

FATHER CALLAHAN

ather Callahan wasn't a fool. Melissa and Tony invited him for dinner every Thursday night because they wanted something. It was obvious so he knew it was Melissa's idea. Still, how could he refuse a wonderful meal with fine wine followed by three games of four-handed pinochle with Olga as his partner. The stakes were high; five dollars a game and a dollar extra every time the losers didn't make their bid. He always left at least ten dollars ahead, and he gladly accepted the bribe although he had no intention of giving in on something so ingrained in his church's system of beliefs. Marriage was sacred and once entered into it could not easily be ended—*What God has joined together, let no man put asunder.* It didn't matter that the man Melissa divorced was bisexual and she found him in the arms of his male lover.

When the good Father learned that Melissa was seeking a divorce he begged her to reconsider. "Your marriage can be saved if you and your husband pray for God's help." When Melissa responded with contempt he warned her, "You will one-day regret getting a divorce. If you remarry, you'll be living in an eternal state of sin unable to receive Holy Communion in the church that baptized you and buried your parents."

Much had changed since Melissa's divorce. She had an infant daughter whose father was dead; she had agreed to marry Tony; and two prominent men had been murdered. Although Melissa despised him, she knew Monsignor Lessari would have broken every rule to marry her and Tony properly, in a Roman Catholic Church. Even Father Callahan knew the Monsignor would have married them.

Although Tony liked Father Callahan and had reasons to stay in his good graces, he didn't care where or how Melissa married him. "Priest, minister or a judge, I don't give a damn who marries us."

There were few people Tony trusted as much as he did Olga. During World War Two she continued to fight the Germans in defense of her once beautiful city, Leningrad, even after her entire family had been killed by them. Melissa, the three children and Tony had become her new family and she would stand with them against any threat. She would also help them as she did when she chided the Priest during their card game. "You're a good man, but you never had a wife and family. It's not natural. In Russia, our priests marry and have many children. And before they marry they sleep with women until they find love—then they marry. You should find a woman. Then you will understand Melissa and find a way to marry her and Tony."

Father Callahan enjoyed the barbs that would have offended a less worldly priest. They reminded him of his time in the army joking with the other men before the Korean War broke out. It was a wonderful two-year period that ended with the start of the war. Fighting, killing and the humiliation of retreat in the face of fresh Chinese troops changed the twenty-year-old kid from Pennsylvania. By the time the fighting ended he had been wounded twice, had received a battlefield promotion to sergeant and had stained his soul with the blood of men killed in combat. He also internalized a deep guilt for the women and children slaughtered in their frantic efforts to flee the war while he and his comrades engaged the enemy.

Melissa could see that his mind had taken him to another place, so she asked, "How well did you know Monsignor Lessari?"

Because Tony knew of their relationship, the good Father glanced his way for a moment before saying, "His death was a horrible tragedy … I miss him. His sense of humor, his advice and his commitment to God and the Church inspired me. He recognized the shortcomings of the Church yet his love and loyalty to it were unwavering." Once again, he looked at Tony before adding, "The Monsignor and I were good friends. We played poker two or three times a month and frequently went to religious retreats together."

It was the perfect opportunity for Melissa. "You should ignore the rules of your Church and marry us. That's what the Monsignor would have done. Once the wedding is over, even the Pope couldn't undo it!"

He responded with a weak smile and again looked at Tony. Father Callahan knew Tony would also eventually try to weaken his resolve. It would be forceful and difficult for him to resist because Tony knew of his love for gambling, women, alcohol and the finer things in life—desires he shared with Monsignor Lessari while they privately ridiculed their Church. And yet they both loved the Church—*Their Church.* As if he were reading his thoughts, Tony said, "Come Father, I have some cognac I'd like you to try." The card game had ended so they left the table and walked to Tony's office, a room so secure that even Olga and Melissa had never set foot inside of it.

Once the password was entered into the code protected lock they entered the room. The good Father glanced around and tried not to show his interest in the artwork, weapons and displays of wealth. The oil paintings of Mary and of the Archangel Gabriel were the best he had ever seen. And only Tony would have four Russian rifles and three Italian made hand guns prominently displayed next to the religious paintings. The weapons were meant for more than display.

He knew Tony would try to force him into violating the rules of the Church and perform the marriage ceremony. "President Kennedy's family had Church marriages after they were divorced, so give Melissa and me the same deal they got."

It wasn't the first time Father Callahan had been reminded of the inconsistencies in applying the Church's rules. His guts twisted when he replied, "They were married in the Church only after their marriages were first annulled, and ..."

"Annulled! Yeah, they were divorced by the Church and the bishop got a bag of money. Annulled, divorced ... same fucking thing, only annulments produce income from the wealthy and powerful. The Church acts like a whore and you're one of its pimps!"

Only in private would Tony degrade him and his Church. Only in private would the Priest allow it without responding in kind, or with violence. But the room was Tony's sanctuary, a place where his strength seemed to intensify. A statue of a black angel with a strange unholy look about it suddenly seized the Priest's attention, as did the stiletto resting next to it. He picked it up and Tony immediately said, "The blade is razor sharp, and she won't protect you."

He confirmed its sharpness and touched the angel's cheek with the tip of the blade. He noted it was a push button knife made in Italy, the kind popular with young street thugs and Italian criminals. For them it was a symbol of their perceived masculinity. The good Father laughed inwardly because he knew how to kill with a knife and suspected that Tony did as well. He recalled how during the Korean War communist troops would quietly cross the battlefield under the cover of darkness and cut the throats of American soldiers while they slept in foxholes. He paid them back, killing many of them, some during combat with a bayonet and others after they had surrendered. He recalled every prisoner of war he killed with a sudden bayonet thrust to the chest. *An eye for an eye* he reasoned, although later he would look back on the killings he was responsible for, even those that took place during combat, with enormous guilt. Despair and guilt so deep that it drove him into the priesthood. Still holding it he said, "This doesn't seem like the kind of knife you would use, Tony."

"I wouldn't."

"Why then is it on display?"

"To complete the scene. To complement my dark angel."

It was beautiful and obscene. The statue of an angel cast in bronze was unlike any the Priest had ever seen. It was deep gray, nearly black. The art dealer shrugged and with a laugh said, "It was made in Heaven or Hell, take your pick," when Tony asked him who made it and where it came from. It was a provocative representation of an angel with wings partially extended, her body barely covered with a shawl-like garment, nipples prominent and pointed beyond reason and an evil smile on her face. She was a dark and unholy angel.

Father Callahan wanted forgiveness for his evil deeds. Yet his urge to gamble, his drinking and his fondness for women harmed no one, though they were inconsistent with his vows as a priest. He studied the statue too long. "You like women, don't you?" Tony asked.

"At least I'm not queer." He continued staring at her.

"I bought all your gambling debts."

"I know. I'll pay them off; I always do."

"Just a run of bad luck?"

"Something like that." He took the glass of cognac Tony handed him. Their glasses tapped softly and the drinks were thrown back.

Tony handed him a bottle of beer. "I expect a hundred dollars a month from now until you pay me off."

It would force him to live a life of poverty. He had no choice, so he nodded his reluctant agreement. The Priest paused briefly and, in a halting voice said, "I'll need a loan so I can win the money I owe you."

The simmering conflict with the Irish and the need to stop one of them from becoming President of the United States was always with Tony. He would need the help of others if he could in any way influence the outcome of their efforts, and a priest, even an Irish priest with a name like Callahan, would be useful if he could be corrupted. There was no doubt Father Callahan was a "worldly man." It was Tony's hope he would become an evil man.

The weekly poker game in Big George's garage started five years earlier and had evolved significantly since then. George bought the garage expecting to use it for a storage locker business. When that failed he capitalized on the high ceilings and built a small indoor basketball court that he and his friends used during the winter months. Beer was consumed in large quantities during the games and there were always a few friends who stayed around afterward for more. Wednesdays were George's day off from work and he encouraged his friends to stay and play cards. Before long the poker game became a tradition, but only those invited by George and Tony, charter members of the game, could attend. Marty Jones was a graduate student in accounting who served in Viet Nam, as did his brother who died there during the Tet offensive. Bill Fern was also a graduate student, majoring in journalism. Two years earlier, during his senior year, Bill was the middle weight collegiate wrestling champ. He hoped to become a sports writer for a major newspaper.

When Tony suggested that Father Callahan be invited to the poker game George exploded. "A priest—are you nuts, Martino!"

"He's not a typical priest," Tony replied. Then he added, "He's a priest like Monsignor Lessari. In fact, they were good friends. Listen, the guy fought in the Korean War, so we should at least give him a chance."

Having never met him, George was confused and surprised, especially hearing that a priest had once been in combat. "Huh. You're sure he'd fit in ... What about Paula Mary? The other guys won't be happy if things change with her—Hell, I won't be happy if things change with her!"

"I said he was like the Monsignor. He'll be alright with Paula Mary."

Paula Mary was a thirty-five-year-old waitress at Diamond Lil's. Her husband was a high school teacher who wasn't all that interested in making love to his wife. Outside of the home, however, he was constantly after females and more than once had sex with a high school girl and got away with it. Paula Mary responded by satisfying her sexual desires with a limited number of men she felt safe with and who were willing to pay for her services. It was an arrangement that worked surprisingly well. In the process, she came into contact with Tony, a generous young man with a lot of money and friends who were influential. He quickly became a frequent customer.

Paula Mary prepared and served food and drinks while the five men played poker. At times, she would deal the cards and occasionally she played a few hands. Tony and George paid her for her time and the winners always gave her a tip when the game ended. For a price, she provided sexual favors after the game, although on frequent occasions a player couldn't wait that long. Monsignor Lessari was the only player who ever tried to stiff her. It didn't matter because she knew Tony would pay the bill and it only happened on those rare occasions when the Monsignor joined the group.

Father Callahan had been playing cards with the group for more than a year and had never asked Paula Mary to join him in the back room after the poker game. He also did his best to ignore it when the others engaged her services. His desire for alcohol and the thrill of gambling were easily rationalized by him. Yet it placed him into an environment where he could easily fulfill the strongest forbidden desires that were within him. At times, they swept over him even as he gave communion to beautiful women, including Paula Mary. It was a world filled with contradictions and dishonesty; and he often thought of his own, even as he forgave those who came to the confessional to ask forgiveness for theirs.

THE FAMILY

———◆———

hey were driving from Wellsboro to Lock Haven on a Tuesday evening. Fall colors were beginning to show adding to the experience as they traveled from one pocket valley to the next. There was the hint of burning wood in the air, but it wasn't natural. A neighbor was careless while burning leaves and a home had caught fire. Expecting to watch the fire consume the structure, the Martino clan: Tony, Melissa, Olga and the three children, left their vehicle and walked slowly toward the flames. A couple stood crying while in a desperate embrace. Barely heard above the fire's noise she sobbed, "My baby." Before long, her husband bolted and ran into the raging flames.

Melissa wrapped her arms around one of Tony's and dug her nails in. Olga did the same with his other arm and noticed the tortured look on his face. A propane tank at the rear of the house exploded. Knowing time was important, Tony began to count softly and deliberately. "One, two, three …" His eyes found the wife's deep blue eyes in an instant of anguish, "eight, nine, ten …" A high-pitched scream and again their eyes locked … "thirteen, fourteen …" Still looking at him she stepped slowly forward … "eighteen, nineteen …" She walked slowly into the inferno and Tony stopped counting.

Only the soft hum of the engine could be heard as they returned to their mountaintop retreat. Melissa carried Sarah, and the two boys followed her to the second-floor bedrooms. Olga put a bottle of cognac on the dining room table along with two glasses and a bottle of beer.

She filled Tony's glass with cognac and put two fingers in hers. "Drink, it'll help." He stared at the crucifix and pulled the glass closer to him.

He drank most of it. She filled it again and then opened the bottle of beer. "They are in the arms of God, together as a family."

He stared at the crucifix before suddenly hurling his glass at Jesus. Olga made the sign of the cross from right to left, the Russian Orthodox way. He picked up the bottles of beer and cognac and glanced at the painting of Mary. Contempt stirred his rage. "God will bless and keep them," Olga said.

"There is no God!" His soul had suddenly changed. He was liberated as his anger and hate turned into a bitter river within him. In the past darkness had come to him when he was provoked. Now it was more intense, more focused, and it had the feel of permanence.

A half moon, the shining river below, and the smell of swamp decay awaited him as he walked away from the house, away from the oak tree he loved, to the edge of the forest. The cognac and beer were clouding his thinking yet he could still see her piercing blue eyes. Her pain was clear as was her hopelessness. The evil within him became stronger, and he embraced it.

Clouds moving in from the west gradually enveloped the moon while fog began to lift from the swamp and drift toward him. A distant sound high in the trees was followed by the slow powerful flight of the predator bird. More cognac. More beer. Anger was still at its zenith, but without the sharp edges. A dark decision was made; he would henceforth kill with no remorse—the way he believed God had killed the blue-eyed woman and her family. The pitiful squeal of a rabbit caught his attention. The outline of the evil bird was barely visible as it carried its prey off into a deep place in the forest. The moon left the sky and the foul-smelling swamp fog made seeing difficult. Using his instincts, he walked blindly to the home hoping to find a sweet evil there and in the haziness of his mind. The interior of the house was dark, his office darker, yet he knew she waited for him; as she had for other men; as she had throughout the ages. He fell into his chair knowing she was near. She was waiting for him, or so he believed.

His eyes closed and his breathing slowed and became shallow; and he entered a state between sleep and awareness. Time passed and he reached for her with his thoughts. He heard her move close to him and thought he felt her sharp nipples press into his chest. She whispered to him, "There is nothing for you in goodness. Accept me, for I alone can protect you and those you love against all things from the light and the darkness." For a time, she slowly moved up and down over the length of his body … before returning to her world.

The next morning Tony awoke and stumbled into the office's bathroom with the encounter fresh in his mind. He looked back into the office and could see on the table the dark bronze angel and the stiletto next to it. It was a dream he would never forget; yet he wondered if it was really just a creation of his imagination. He could still feel pain in his chest, as if she were still pressing her body into his.

Conversations at breakfast were subdued. The children said nothing about the fire and the adults were glad for it. Melissa served him a cup of coffee and said, "You'll be OK." Then she softly kissed his cheek. After everyone finished eating, Tony helped her clean the table while Olga watched over the children in the living room. When Tony brushed up against her, Melissa moved far enough away to make her feelings known. "Are you playing poker tonight?" she asked.

"Yeah, it's Wednesday night, so I'll be late." He replied, as he thought about the women who had satisfied him in the past; about the murders he had committed; and about the deaths of the innocent child and mother. The father who died while trying to save his child also came to mind, and Tony asked his dark angel to comfort all of them.

Tony arrived at the card game early hoping that Paula would be there eager to earn some money and fill the void left by Melissa's latest rejection. The door to the rear room was closed and a dim light could be seen at the bottom of the door. He removed his shirt, shoes and trousers and waited as his thought of the way the wife looked at him with her piercing blue eyes. His anger grew knowing it would make the love making more intense. He slowly stood when the door opened. Father Callahan just nodded and moved to the side so Tony could walk by. Paula had a fondness for Tony and immediately knew he needed the comfort only a woman's body could provide. She knelt on the bed, extended her arms to him, and they slowly embraced. He winced when her breasts pressed against him. There was an unusual taste when they kissed and his tongue was warmer than any she had ever experienced. Their love making was aggressive and she tasted his blood. When they finished she applied a lotion to the small puncture like wounds on his muscular chest.

Paula quietly prepared the room for the poker game and Tony took his usual seat. When she placed a bottle of cognac on the small table next to him, he said, "I'll be drinking beer tonight, at least in the beginning."

George arrived a short time later followed by Bill and Marty. Bill said they shouldn't start until the Priest showed up because he had been the big winner the previous week. The game began as soon as Father Callahan arrived and after a couple hours it seemed like he would again be the big winner.

A little before 2 AM, George received a strange call from the guy who managed Diamond Lil's for him on Wednesdays. Someone called asking for George saying he had a big story for the newspaper. The manager called to say he gave the caller George's number at the poker game. Moments after he hung up the telephone it rang again and George answered. He was dumbfounded by what he heard. "Tony, I don't know if this is real or not. The call …" He paused to catch his breath. "The guy said your cousin Joey was gunned down by a friend of Judge Archer. Said he saw it happen about an hour ago, in a coal field near North Slope. Then he slammed down the phone."

"Call the police!"

"How? Who? It must have happened outside of North Slope—that's about a hundred miles from here. I don't know who to call."

"Call Carl, he's the county Sheriff. He'll know who to contact back in North Slope," Bill answered.

Tony slowly shuffled the cards while George called the Clinton County Sheriff. When George was finished he told the group, "The Sheriff said he'll contact the State Police and we should all stay right here."

Tony grabbed the telephone from George's hand and called his father, Frank Martino.

"Pop, I'm sorry to wake you, but this can't wait."

…

"I'm playing cards with George and three other guys. George just got a call from someone saying Joey was shot, somewhere out in a coal field. Sometimes he works late fixing trucks and mining equipment in that old garage he owns near the Dolly Gray stripping hole."

…

"Yeah, look into it and get back to me. Another thing. The caller said a friend of Judge Archer did it."

…

"I know, I know. Just call me when you learn something."

Tony continued shuffling the cards … very slowly, as if they were speaking to him. "Are you OK?" Father Callahan asked. Tony had a puzzled look on his face and looked at each of the men as he continued to handle the cards.

"Hey Tony," George said, "maybe you should wait in Paula's room in the back until the police show up."

He looked at Paula for a short time before saying, "Everyone ante up five dollars … one hand of five card straight poker with no draw."

They were all confused by Tony's behavior. He slid the cards to his right and asked Bill to cut the deck. Then he slowly passed out the cards, one by one, going around the table five times. George turned his cards over first: a pair of sevens. Father Callahan was next: two pairs, fives and jacks. Marty had queen high and Bill had a pair of nines. All eyes turned to Tony. He turned his cards over one at a time: ace of spades, queen of spades, ace of diamonds, ace of clubs, and ace of hearts. Four aces. "Yeah, I'm OK," he answered. He picked up the twenty-five dollars and gave it to Paula. "The deck is marked."

It didn't take George long to figure it out. "You son-of-a-bitch!" He shouted, as he put the full strength of his three-hundred-pound body into a right fist that nearly tore Father Callahan's head off. Bill and Marty joined George in kicking and punching the Priest while Tony watched. They stopped when Paula came to his aid, covering his body with hers. The Priest's money was divided up and the game resumed.

"Help me carry him to the back room," Paula pleaded.

"Let him lick his wounds right there, like a dirty dog," Marty answered. Marty was *Protestant Irish* and didn't care much for Roman Catholic priests. Knowing Tony no longer respected Catholic men with black and white collars, he got along well with him and other *lip service* Catholics. Paula helped Father Callahan move to the side of the room.

When the Sheriff arrived, he looked at the Priest and Paula on the side of the room and the four men playing cards. "Ask no questions and you'll hear no lies," Bill bellowed. He got the message, sat down and said, "Deal me in. Someone will show up from the State Police when they figure out what the hell is going on."

By the time Tony's father called back, the Sheriff and George were up over one hundred dollars each.

"Is he dead?" Tony immediately asked.

... .

"Blood on the outside of his car, nothing else?"

...

"More blood in the undergrowth and a blood trail ... but no body?"

...

"Hell, maybe they didn't kill him."

...

"Recent blast in a mine vent hole ... So, some of the cops think the body was dumped into it and then it was sealed with dynamite."

...

"You don't think so."

...

"You think they put him in an abandoned car and pushed it into the stripping hole ... I remember swimming there as a kid. That thing's deep and there's probably a hundred cars in there—I'll bet there's more than a few bodies in there, too."

...

"I understand ... because they found fresh blood on the ground near the stripping."

...

"I know, I know. Don't worry, justice will be done."

...

"Listen Pop, in this world or next, there will be justice ... I know, you want it in this world."

...

"You guarantee it ... I get it, just be careful."

Once they completed their preliminary investigation, it would take at least two hours for the State Police officers who conducted the investigation to drive from North Slope to Lock Haven, so the game resumed. Paula went out for donuts and made coffee. After she returned she sat with the Priest as he rested against the wall and drank whiskey with his donut.

Shortly after sunrise the thunder of an explosion shook the card table. Seconds later another larger explosion brought all of them to their feet. The Sheriff knocked over his chair as he rushed from the room leaving his winnings behind. The other card players, their emotions dampened by alcohol, the late hour and the still unfolding events sat nervously for a moment before George roared, "What in the hell was that?"

"The sound of justice," Tony replied. Then, he looked at the Priest and added, "I suppose you can call it that."

Gasoline from two well-thrown dynamite fire-bombs ignited a blaze that quickly consumed the historic home. After the fire marshal ruled that the site was safe, the police found the remains of two children and their parents. The parents were courthouse employees: an assistant district attorney and his wife, an accountant. They had been friends of Judge Archer.

The poker game continued on Wednesday nights with the four remaining players. Carol, Melissa's sister, replaced Paula although she didn't offer the sexual services Paula had provided. The five of them grew close and quickly became the brains behind George's expanding and rapidly evolving newspaper. However, Bill, Marty and Tony didn't work for the newspaper and would never acknowledge any relationship with it.

Since she was a young girl Carol sought out excitement and adventure. Yet it came as a surprise when she asked if she could write articles, perhaps even a column, for the newspaper. She was interested in the dark side of society: crime, political corruption and especially sexual abuse of children that was beginning to surface in her church. She was certain that newspapers and other sources for the news had conspired with powerful interests to withhold information from the public that could threaten the status quo. Hearing of her interest in writing, Tony responded with a small laugh and a smile. Then he suggested she write under a pen name; a name he called her by during their private moments—*Dark Angel*.

THE INTERROGATION

---•◆•---

Judge Archer once described Tony Martino as a cross between Leonardo Da Vinci and Attila the Hun, so he should have known better than to enter into a prolonged conflict with Tony. Was it the money or, as some believed, did he simply think his position as senior judge in Clinton County, Pennsylvania made him a God-like figure beyond the reach of an Italian criminal. Tony was brilliant, violent and had never been convicted of a crime. As far as the Judge knew he had never distinguished himself at anything. In contrast, Judge Archer was surrounded by a loyal circle of corrupt politicians and police officers that extended all the way to Harrisburg, the state capital. And he used his influence wisely. A single telephone call from the Judge could produce a job with the Pennsylvania Turnpike Commission, state government, several school districts or with the University located a few blocks from the Judge's home. The recipients of such favors and their families could be counted on in the future when the Judge needed help. The Judge's reach was great and it endured even after his death. The courthouse was staffed almost entirely with people still loyal to the Judge, although they were rattled by the firebombing that had taken the lives of two of them.

There were three powerful men in Clinton County: the senior Judge in the courthouse, Tony and the President of the University. Although they were very different, all three used their power and influence to benefit themselves and their friends. When the Judge was murdered something of a vacuum developed in the courthouse. Although he wasn't above taking a bribe, the Sheriff had through the years managed to stay beyond the grasp of the Judge. It was unlikely, but Tony hoped the Sheriff would eventually become the dominant power broker in the courthouse.

Surprisingly, Tony wasn't the one who killed the Judge. Many people thought otherwise because they knew Tony was furious with the Judge because he demanded a monetary bribe before he would allow Tony to adopt a young boy. Eventually Tony was able to adopt Timmy ending his dispute with the Judge. After Tony became the young boy's adoptive father, the Monsignor told Joey Martino, Tony's cousin, to kill Judge Archer if Tony didn't do it. Tony simply didn't see any reason for a killing because he had beaten and humiliated the Judge. When Tony found Joey standing over the Judge's body, gun in hand, he felt a strong urge to kill him. Monsignor Lessari had become a criminal who knowingly reversed a decision made by a killer. In so doing he had crossed the line into Tony's world. Tony had killed men for doing less. It was Tony's call—kill the Judge or let him live. Anyone but a blood relative, Tony would have killed in a heartbeat. Tony left Joey standing over the Judge's body and drove to North Slope, in the heart of hard coal country, knowing the Monsignor was responsible for the Judge's murder. Once there, he brutally killed the Monsignor with his knife— the very knife the Monsignor had blessed for him.

Monsignor Lessari and Judge Archer had much in common. They loved women, good liquor and cards. And like powerful men everywhere they expected their instructions, even their suggestions, to be followed. Judge Archer was involved in a wide range of illegal and unethical activities, something all too common for judges in Pennsylvania. But selling kids from an orphanage to desperate couples who couldn't produce offspring was beyond the pale. Monsignor Lessari wanted Judge Archer dead from the moment he heard the Judge was trying to squeeze money from Tony in exchange for allowing Tony to adopt Timmy, a young disabled boy who shared an incredibly strong bond with Tony.

The three men were silent as they climbed the stairs of the Clinton County Court House. Once they entered the courthouse, those who saw them were also quiet. Tony Martino and his friends—Big George and Ben Sherman, a disbarred Jewish attorney from Philadelphia— were grim and sinister looking. Those who saw Tony, especially the courthouse employees, knew he was there for questioning by the Pennsylvania State Police. Although they didn't recognized Ben, they correctly assumed George and Ben would assist him.

It was a small courthouse and there were few secrets, only the illusion that some information wasn't to be shared. Since Carl Marsit, the county Sheriff, escorted three unknown men to the second-floor meeting room only a few minutes earlier, there were deep concerns. Until he was murdered, Judge Archer held everything together. And like a typical senior county judge he made sure the right people, especially the district attorney and the other judges, received a fair share of the bribe and kickback money that lubricated the wheels of progress and bought silence, loyalty and cooperation from a broad spectrum of county employees and a few who worked for the state. Among those who had supported the Judge, there was fear the investigation into the Judge's death could release the stench of corruption that had benefited a few and harmed many.

"This is Tony Martino. The big guy to his right is George Orvat, an area businessman. On his left is Ben … What's your last name, Ben?" The Sheriff asked, as the three men entered the room.

"It doesn't matter," Tony replied. The Sheriff was sitting at the end of a long table in a sparsely furnished room.

"All right, Tony. Directly across from you is Pennsylvania State Trooper Fred White."

"Let me see your ID." Tony extended his hand as the Trooper reached into the inside pocket of his jacket. He looked like a businessman in a black suit with a gray tie. The patch on his right shoulder identified him as a State Trooper. Like most Troopers, he didn't like the *tin soldier* look of the uniform Pennsylvania State Police officers normally wore.

"This is all bull," the Trooper said to Tony as he handed him his identification. Tony passed it on to George and the Trooper continued,

"There's no need to have witnesses and to tape record everything." George recorded information from the Trooper's identification card and plugged in the tape recorder. "It's just going to slow things down," he added with irritation.

"It's for me, not you!" Tony snapped back. "With a tape of our discussion and two of my friends taking notes, you won't be able to falsely accuse me of obstructing justice or providing false information."

The Sheriff didn't want to be there, but he owed Tony and they were friends. He said, "Tony asked me if it was Ok. I told him there's no law or rule I know of prohibiting taking notes or recording what's said during a police interview. Am I wrong about that, Fred?"

The Trooper ignored the Sheriff and asked Tony a question. "Mister Martino, did you see Judge Archer or Monsignor Lessari the day they were murdered?"

"Yeah, both of them, and they were breathing when I left them … but what about these two guys with you? Who the hell are they?"

"They're just observers. They won't be asking any questions."

"I don't give a shit! Who the hell are they and why are they here?"

Hoping for a few words of support, the Trooper looked at the Sheriff. Instead, the Sheriff said, "Seems like a reasonable request."

Trooper White wasn't happy about the way the investigation into the murder of the two men was being handled. He believed there were too many distractions and knew that FBI and Pennsylvania Crime Commission involvement would only make things worse. When the public became aware of their interest it would make Trooper White's job more difficult, but the FBI and the Crime Commission forced their way into the investigation and he had to live with it, although he didn't need to like it.

The man to the Trooper's right spoke softly. "They don't need to know." The man to his left nodded in approval. Wearing shirts and ties and with crew-cut hair styles, the three men were too rigid. They couldn't blend in with the general population of any rural area in Pennsylvania.

Unlike the other two men, Trooper White didn't care. He wanted to get somewhere with the investigation and knew exactly what he was doing when he said, "This is Henry Johns, he's with the FBI." Then, pointing to his right he added, "That guy is Robert Stokes of the Pennsylvania Crime Commission."

Predictably, Tony looked at the Trooper and said, "I want to see their identifications."

"I don't need to show you mine!" the FBI agent replied.

"Then get the fuck out of here!" Tony stood with his clinched fists on the table. The other men, including Trooper White, remained seated and silent. Tony knew his rights and was prepared to fight for them, physically if necessary. The FBI agent was on his own.

Trooper White crossed his arms and looked at the agent. *I told you so* was written on his face as clearly as the words *Vietnam Veteran* on George's tee shirt.

"You're losing control here, Trooper White," the agent said. Then he found his ID and placed it in front of Tony. First George, then Ben recorded information from the ID. The Crime Commission investigator presented his ID and the process was repeated. Although Trooper White had questioned many suspects during his 23 years in the Pennsylvania State Police, he had never been involved in anything like this.

"Son of a bitch!" Sheriff Marsit said under his voice before he settled into a chair at the end of the table. He knew it would be a long meeting that would likely produce echoes for the following months. He could live without that.

Q: For the record, Mister Martino, give me your complete name and place of residence.

A: Tony Martino, Lock Haven, Pennsylvania, Dead Indian Swamp Road.

Q: You knew Judge Archer, didn't you?

A: Yeah, since I was a sophomore at the University.

Q: Did you see him the day he was murdered?

A: Yes.

Q: What time was it?

A: Not sure … in the morning … probably around 10 AM … could have been later.

Q: Did the two of you argue?

A: No, no reason to.

Q: You went to see him at his cabin on Pine Creek. Is that right?

A: Yes.

Q: Why? For what purpose?

A: Two reasons. First, to return a pistol.

Q: A pistol!

A: If you found it at the scene, my prints will be on it. It was his father's and I borrowed it, so I wanted to return it.

Q: The other reason?

A: I asked him to give his wife the director's job at the orphanage.

The Trooper was confused so he looked at the Sheriff. "The Judge had his fingers into a lot of things. Believe me, he could have arranged for her to get the job."

Q: OK, the Judge could have arranged it. But you asking him to hire his wife sounds strange; especially since you were sleeping with her.

A: Sure, and he knew it. But she had kicked him out because he had a girlfriend, and not his first.

Q: Did she know you were asking the Judge to give her a job?

A: No, but we talked about her running the orphanage. She loved kids and I knew she'd be good at it.

The Sheriff interrupted. "She is good at it. She got the job shortly after the Judge was killed."

Q: You sleeping with his wife. There must have been a lot of hate between you and the Judge.

A: Yeah, but we got past it. There was another issue, too.

Q: Which was?

A: The Judge gave me a hassle; made it hard for me to adopt my son Timmy.

Once again, the Trooper looked at the Sheriff who nodded to support what Tony had said.

Q: You don't seem like a forgiving kind of guy, Mister Martino. Do you expect me to believe you didn't hate the Judge, probably enough to kill him?

A: I don't give a fuck what you believe—I didn't kill him! ... Besides, I hate a lot of people *enough to kill them* which doesn't mean a damn thing.

Q: So, who did kill him?

A: Do you want facts or opinions—because I don't have any direct knowledge.

Q: OK then, opinions.

A: If the Judge died first, and that's the rumor I heard, I think the Monsignor had the Judge killed, and then one of the Judge's friends retaliated by killing the Monsignor.

The Trooper had heard it before and hoped it was true. It would make his life much easier. But the FBI and the Crime Commission weren't buying into it because it would end there, all nice and neat. They believed there wasn't any evidence to support the tit-for-tat killings scenario. The FBI and the Commission had their own agendas, so Trooper White continued.

Q: A Monsignor having a Judge killed, seems unlikely.

A: They hated each other. Ask the Sheriff.

The Sheriff replied, "That's true. I saw the Monsignor attack the Judge during a party at Tony's home. Beat the Judge real good. Would have killed him, if Tony's family hadn't stopped him."

"Oh God," the Trooper sighed, as he wrote some notes and tried to get a handle on what Tony said. He had heard some of it from other sources, but a priest beating a judge—it seemed like a hard coal country myth.

Q: Any other opinions about the Judge's killing?

A: Yeah, a few more. I'll summarize it all down to this: Judge Archer had a lot of enemies and he deserved them. Any one of them could have killed him.

Q: Give me a break. We're talking about murder here; give me more than street rumors.

A: All right. The Judge was on a weekend fishing trip with his friend, Jason Dorman. His friend disappeared and his body was never found. Now that's a fact.

Q: And?

A: The Judge killed him and disposed of the body.

Q: Why?

Tony delayed. It was the question he was hoping for, but he didn't want it to seem easy or that he was eager. With the Judge dead and his Cousin Joey and his girlfriend missing, Tony was the only one who really knew what had happened to Jason Dorman.

Q: Mister Martino, why would the Judge kill Jason Dorman?

Even the Sheriff and Tony's other friends, George and Ben, held their breaths while waiting for an answer.

A: They were selling kids from the orphanage and there were problems between them and with other people about the split. That's why the Judge killed him.

The Sheriff became angry. "Jesus, Tony, why didn't you tell me about this?"

"Why? You work in this fucking courthouse, so maybe you're part of it."

Suddenly some of the pieces were coming together for Trooper White.

Q: Your son Timmy … you had to pay the Judge for him, didn't you?

A: Yeah, and I didn't like it one fucking bit.

Q: Selling kids, especially selling Timmy to you, that's why the Monsignor hated the Judge.

A: Absolutely … seems like a good reason to me.

Q: Do you have any evidence to support what you've said?

A: What do you expect, a goddamn receipt? I don't, but people in the courthouse do. Hell, they almost certainly got some of the money, including some of my money.

"Let's take a break," the Trooper suddenly announced. He, the FBI agent and Crime Commission investigator left the room and began a heated discussion in the hallway.

The Sheriff had hoped Tony wouldn't see it. The investigator, a Pennsylvania State Trooper prior to joining the Crime Commission, left a candy wrapper on the table.

Only Ben remained silent while an equally heated discussion took place in the meeting room. George had only recently started a newspaper and could smell a story that could quickly turn it into a financial success. "Tony, Carl, tell me who I can talk to. How can I get to the bottom of this selling orphanage kids racket? … Goddammit, somebody's got to know about it!"

"Run a story with what you got … Tie it into the Judge's murder and the Monsignor's," Tony replied.

"You can't do that!" the Sheriff shouted. "But if you do, leave me out of it."

Then Tony picked up the candy wrapper and said, "This is the same wrapper we found on my property."

"I know Tony, but that doesn't mean much. He's not the only person who eats that candy."

"Like hell! He's one of the guys who illegally entered my property and stole a gold coin. For his own good, you better tell him I want it back!"

Confusion. Distractions. It was what Tony wanted. Not only would it make it more difficult for the investigation to go forward. If he or any of his family and friends were ever charged with anything related to the killings, he would have created doubt and sympathy in the minds of potential jurors. Even cops and prosecutors in and around Clinton County and hard coal country would be sympathetic to anyone who stood up to a corrupt judge and his friends who were in the business of selling kids. Especially if they killed a priest who tried to stop them.

George knew nothing about the candy wrapper or the missing gold coin and he was writing notes and talking at the same time. "Who do I talk to at the courthouse, and Sheriff, for the record, what's Tony talking about? Did one of those cops steal something valuable from Tony? … Oh God, what a story this will make!"

"Just wait," Tony said, while looking over George's notes. "Wait until I tell this cop what I know about Joey and the Monsignor. Then you'll have a real story, George."

The Sheriff was nervous and said, "Now this is serious stuff, Tony. Lying to this guy will blow up in your face."

"I'm going to tell it straight. What are you worried about Carl, if you didn't have anything to do with it? Hell, your job as Sheriff is safe … I know you Carl, as well as I knew the Judge. Maybe you didn't take any money from selling kids, but you knew about it. You HAD to know about it!"

Carl stared at the other three men for the longest while. Then he said, "Ben, would you mind leaving the room for a little while?" Ben knew he wasn't part of Tony's inner circle of friends. He left the room expecting that one day he would be.

They had been friends for years—drinking, playing cards, womanizing and at times engaging in illegal activities. Tony once paid off a poor farmer after Carl beat his son for drunk driving, and George sold stolen liquor and jewelry at his bar. Tony saw to it that George's bar, Diamond Lil's, got the merchandise and Carl often bought some of it. All of that was common for police officers in Pennsylvania, but it paled in comparison to selling children or killing.

Carl sat down across from the other two and said, "Look guys, I heard rumors about a lot of stuff going on here, but how far do you think I'd get investigating any of it. Sure I'm elected, but the judges, especially Judge Archer, called the shots here. Unless he or one of the other judges approved of it, I couldn't get anywhere looking into illegal activities here at the courthouse."

"What about selling kids?" George snapped. "Did you hear anything?"

"If I say anything, are you going to put it in your damn newspaper?"

It was a good question and George had to think about it before answering, so Tony replied, "Couldn't you write your article and just cite sources that asked for the protection of remaining anonymous?"

George liked the idea because it would give the impression that danger and secrecy surrounded the story. It would also allow George to do what many newspapers did—create facts where none existed and do it under the protection of *freedom of the press*. Yes, George liked it.

Before the Sheriff could finish *spilling his guts* to George, the other three men returned to the room and Trooper White once again began to question Tony.

Q: The day of the killings, how many times did you travel from North Slope to the Judge's cabin?

A: Once to the cabin and twice to North Fork ... Went to see Joey in North Fork then traveled back along the same road, most of the way, to see the Judge. After that I went back to North Fork to see the Monsignor.

Q: That doesn't make sense. Lock Haven to North Slope doesn't ...

A: I know it's not the most direct route, but it's a beautiful drive, so I often go that way. And after seeing the Judge I returned to North Slope so the Monsignor could hear my confession.

Q: Confession my ass! ... We'll get back to that later. It just seems like you did a hell of a lot of unnecessary driving.

A: I guess, but I had a lot to think over. The long drive gave me time to think.

Q: Why did you go to see Joey?

A: OK, but tell me who was murdered first—the Judge or the Monsignor? I think it was the Judge, because that makes sense to me. Then the Judge's friends killed the Monsignor and later Joey.

Trooper White wasn't sure how to answer Tony's questions … Then George replied, "He doesn't know! That's why he's not answering. He just DOES NOT know."

Q: Now listen for a minute. The killings took place in the same time frame and there was a major storm, and then a fire at the Judge's cabin added to the confusion. For now, let's say I'm not sure which killing took place first. But your ideas all revolve around the Judge being killed first and the Monsignor later.

Tony knew that was exactly what happened, but he wanted to test the Trooper's understanding of events and also wanted to give himself some room to maneuver, in case he became a suspect in either killing.

Q: Ok, I'll ask you again. Why did you go to see Joey?

Tony remained silent, as if he were reluctant to answer.

Q: Now that's a simple straight forward question Mr. Martino. Why did you see Joey?
A: Joey told me by telephone that he had solid evidence linking the Judge to the selling of children from the orphanage. I wanted to know more … I wanted to see it. He wouldn't budge. He said he would share it with the Monsignor, and only if he agreed would I ever get to see it.

There it was, evidence, or at least the possibility of evidence, that would help explain the killings.

Q: You never saw the evidence?
A: No.
Q: You have no idea what it consisted of?
A: No. But it was clear to me that Joey and the Monsignor were cooking something up.
Q: After you got nowhere with Joey, you went to see Judge Archer.

A: Right.

Q: Then you returned to see the Monsignor?

A: Yes.

Q: You said before it was for confession—that's a lot of bull! You went back to see him so you could find out about the evidence.

A: Yeah, I guess that's obvious, isn't it?

Q: Did he show it to you or tell you what it was?

A: No. We argued about it but he wouldn't tell me a damn thing, except ...

Q: Except what?

A: He told me to go home. He said he and Joey would take care of it.

Q: Take care of it. That meant they would kill the Judge!

A: Yeah, but I didn't realize it at the time. Hell, this was a Roman Catholic Priest telling me he would take care of it. I thought he meant going to the police.

Q: Your cousin Joey is missing ...

A: He's dead.

Q: We're not sure of that; there's no body.

A: Bull. It all fits and you know it. Joey probably did the killing for the Monsignor. Then Judge Archer's friends killed the Monsignor and later they got Joey. It all fits.

Q: If it all fits—where's the evidence?

A: I have no idea. Where's your evidence, or are you protecting the Judge and his friends?

Q: The night you got the call that Joey was shot ...

A: I didn't get the call, George did.

George: That's right.

Sheriff: Then George called me and I called the State Police barracks near North Slope.

It was coming together too early, yet the three investigators couldn't imagine how events could have taken place the way Tony was describing them. In fact, they hoped he was wrong. The Trooper was duty bound, however, to consider any evidence that could support Tony's story.

Q: And where were you from the time George received the call until the bombing?

A: Four of us were playing cards when the call came in. I never left the room. Hell, I never left the chair.

George: There were four of us in the room with Tony … no, five.

Sheriff: I can vouch for that. I showed up shortly after George called me and stayed until the explosions went off.

Q: And Joey, the guy with the evidence, vanishes after he was reported shot. We keep circling back … where's the evidence? … There simply IS NOT any evidence to support what you're telling me.

A: Evidence! You don't want to solve any of this which is probably why you haven't found any evidence. If the three of you got off your asses and started to look you'd find something. If you want evidence—how about the bodies, the telephone call and the bombing of the house? And if you start digging, you'll find evidence that the Judge was selling kids from the orphanage and that people in this very building were part of it.

Q: And the bombing of the house … Why? … Who did it?

A: It's obvious, isn't it? Payback for killing Joey.

As the interrogation ended, Trooper White's head was spinning. All he had were Tony's theories about the killings and the possible murder of Joey Martino. Adding to his concerns was the mad dash George made for the district attorney's office. It was now clear to the Trooper that George was a newspaper reporter and he was going to begin questioning Clinton County courthouse employees about Tony's accusations.

The next day, the headline in George's paper were all that Tony hoped for and what the Sheriff and Trooper feared.

Courthouse Corruption
State Police and FBI are confused ... or are they part of it?

Other Pennsylvania newspapers, especially those in the hard coal region, began to follow the story. Within a few weeks George's newspaper was well known and widely quoted. Then it happened. George received an anonymous telephone call telling him to examine the contents of a small box that could be found on the kitchen table of the deer camp that he, Tony and several of their friends owned. Inside was a blood covered rock and a blood covered knife in separate plastic bags. A typed note in the box simply stated: *Jason Dorman attacked Judge Archer with the rock. The Judge killed him with the knife and disposed of his body.*

After photographing the rock and knife and copying the note, George called Sheriff Marsit and turned the evidence over to him.

The next day George's newspaper printed ten thousand extra copies and newsstands clamored for more. Lost on the second page were words of caution. "How can we be sure these articles are genuine or a hoax?" Yet the knife, rock and note were consistent with the testimony Tony gave. Trooper White's words of caution were ignored. However, two weeks later the crime lab released its findings: *finger prints on the knife were Judge Archer's, and the blood matched that of Dorman when compared to his medical records.*

Efforts to find Joey's body came to a halt although blood found at the scene where he was reported to have been shot was his blood type. Because his girlfriend, Samantha, vanished the same night Joey was reported shot, another layer was added to the mystery.

Trooper White had only Tony's testimony along with the bloody rock and an equally bloody knife, both of which were provided by George. The Trooper knew he had six definite killings and as many as three other possible killings. Yet he believed he had too little evidence, but someone provided George with the rock, knife and note—and although they hadn't been identified, they could certainly fill in many of the blanks, if they wanted to. And ironically, all the evidence he had before him supported the opinions Tony had voiced earlier.

Although they were initially reluctant, parents of five children adopted from the orphanage came forth with stories consistent with Tony's testimony. They paid Judge Archer or one of his cronies for their child. They had been silent out of fear that their child would be taken from them either by Judge Archer's friends or by a state agency, because the adoption was the result of a bribe.

George's newspaper increased the intensity and frequency of its attacks on state and federal law enforcement agencies, including the FBI. Shortly afterward, the Pennsylvania Crime Commission released a report in which it concluded that Tony was a member of a crime family and George was an associate of that family. George was furious and attacked the Commission and those working for it with language rarely seen in newspapers: *Nazi bastards, Storm Troopers, thugs on the state payroll and cowards unwilling to give honest Americans a chance to defend themselves in court before a judge and jury.*

George had a lot of support. Newspapers and civil libertarians had long opposed the tactics used by the Commission. Because the Commission's behavior was eroding public confidence in the criminal justice system, police officers, prosecutors and judges also spoke out against it.

Several weeks had passed and public interest in the murders was waning. Then, after receiving another anonymous telephone call, George received a single piece of paper in the mail connecting the Judge to the selling children scheme. After copying it, he again called Sheriff Marsit and passed it on to him. It listed the names of children sold, their adoptive parents and the amounts paid for each child. Incredibly, the Judge and Jason Dorman, the director of the orphanage until he disappeared, signed the bottom of the page. Dorman was the man Tony said the Judge killed, and his blood and Judge Archer's finger prints were found on the knife previously send to Big George.

The state crime laboratory quickly determined that the document was legitimate. The Judge's fingerprints were on the page and handwriting experts confirmed that it was his signature. It didn't matter much, but the lab also confirmed that Jason Dorman's signature was genuine and that his fingerprints were also on the paper.

George was so excited he nearly exploded. The very next day, his newspaper reported that Tony Martino had figured it all out weeks earlier while the Pennsylvania State Police, the FBI and the Crime Commission tripped over themselves in a failed attempt to involve innocent Italian Americans while protecting crooks who were on the public payroll. Thanks to George and many media outlets, confidence in law enforcement was eroding.

Because the University received substantial funding from the federal government and the Commonwealth of Pennsylvania, University employees rarely became involved in public controversies. Yet many faculty members of the University could no longer remain silent. Not only did they speak out at public forums, some even included the many issues that had been raised in their courses. Not one of them supported the behavior of the Crime Commission, the FBI or the county employees who clearly cooperated with Judge Archer. Not surprisingly, George and Tony became local heroes for standing up to courthouse corruption and for confronting the FBI and the Crime Commission.

George had convinced himself and the public that the two killings had occurred as Tony theorized; the Monsignor had the Judge killed and the Judge's friends had the Monsignor killed. As for Joey, Tony told George that Joey was controlled by the Monsignor so he was the one who probably shot the Judge. The Judge's friends were, in the eyes of the public, becoming a mysterious evil force, thanks to the crimes Tony had attributed to them. Tony also told George that they very likely killed Joey and disposed of his body. By this time, George was becoming a skilled journalist capable of blending the truth with rumors for the purpose of selling newspapers. He told his readers that a reliable source informed him that Judge Archer's friends had killed Joey. George then sweetened the story by adding that Joey also had violent friends who very likely sought revenge by killing courthouse employees. He then went beyond what Tony was telling him. He printed that his sources indicated the killing wasn't over!

It was all too perfect and easy for Trooper White, the FBI and the

Crime Commission. They reluctantly accepted the knife, rock and list of children's names as evidence because they had no other choice. They continued their investigation, yet they knew the only person with direct knowledge about the rash of killings was Tony. And he had given them little information and a lot of speculation. It was also clear that he wasn't going to provide any additional information. Yet too much of his speculation was later supported by evidence that surfaced a few weeks later. People in law enforcement didn't like it. Nevertheless, they were unable to refute anything that Tony had told them.

The Pennsylvania Crime Commission was established in 1968 and was given a mandate to investigate "serious crime wherever it existed in Pennsylvania." The reality behind that generic statement meant that the Commission's mission was to go after Italian criminals. It did that but in a strange way, because while it could investigate, with subpoena power, it lacked the authority to arrest or prosecute. That left it with one tool which it used with a vengeance and with little regard for accuracy or the truth— Pennsylvania Crime Commission Reports.

In spite of its reckless disregard for facts and rights protected by the Constitution, the Commission's annual reports were widely cited by news organizations, also with little regard for accuracy, fair play or individual rights protected by the Constitution. One oft cited example of the Commission's incompetence involved Salvatore Sabella. The Commission reported that he had been "deported," a punishment reserved for criminals the federal government could not convict, but could forcibly return to their home country. For decades "deportation" was used to rid the United States of Nazi war criminals and Italian born crime figures. But Salvatore Sabella had not been deported! He died and was buried outside of Philadelphia, a short distance from the Crime Commission's office! With a staff of fifty, including attorneys and police officers, and a large budget, it routinely failed to even use the public record to check the accuracy of the material presented in its annual reports.

The Commission's record was so bad that it was widely criticized by members of the Pennsylvania Bar, civil libertarians and people in law enforcement. Not surprisingly, the Commission's behavior produced an enormous loss of respect for the criminal justice system, especially among Italian Americans. Yet none of this seemed to matter. What did matter, however, was that the Commission began to investigate the best funded and most highly organized criminals in Pennsylvania—the politicians. The result was predictable, but it took years to play out. The Commission eventually lost state funding.

In spite of the loathing many people had for the Commission, their reports were still cited years after the Commission had ceased to exist, implying that individuals, some of whom had never been convicted of a crime, were in some way connected with organized criminal organizations. In most cases they were Italian Americans.

KILL ONLY LESSER MEN

I t's hard to look past a murder, especially when the victim was President of the United States. A body of respected well known political types had concluded that the assassination was the work of one man acting alone. Yet a few years later another equally qualified group concluded that it was unlikely that only one person was entirely responsible for the killing. Many people, most importantly members of the assassinated President's family, believed it was all too convenient. The President was shot dead and a day later his killer was shot and killed while in police custody, putting a fine point ending to the greatest crime of the 20th century. Adding to the confusion were a host of Italian criminals boasting that they had played a role in the assassination. Most of them were in prison where even the slightest connection to the President's death would make them men to be respected among the rest of the Italian inmate population.

It was widely known that powerful Italian crime family members had played an essential role in the President's campaign to receive his party's nomination; and an equally critical part in his election to the most powerful office in the world. When the President turned on the crime families with aggressive investigations their anger was predictable and deep. Yet the President and his family believed the prestige of the office and a powerful array of law enforcement agencies protecting him would surely make him invulnerable.

A few years after the President's assassination, his brother, the next oldest son in the family, was elected Senator from Connecticut. Before completing his term in office, he decided to run for President. He would have secured the nomination, but he too was assassinated after winning an important presidential primary in Texas. His alleged killer was quickly arrested and convicted. However, the police destroyed evidence during their investigation and although the alleged killer was at the scene of the crime there was an enormous amount of evidence indicating that it was impossible for shots fired from his gun to have killed the Senator. Similarities between the two assassinations were astonishing, especially since the Senator had played a significant role going after Italian criminals while his brother was President and, once again, a host of Italian criminals publicly boasted that they had contributed to the Senator's assassination.

Although they were largely silent about it, family members of the President and Senator believed Italian organized crime figures were responsible for both assassinations, even if the men who actually fired the shots were apprehended. That, and the criminals who boasted about roles they played in the assassinations, not only embarrassed the FBI and other law enforcement agencies, it made it virtually impossible to investigate any suspects when viable clues surfaced regarding either murder.

It was against this backdrop that the third brother, who had been elected Senator from Massachusetts shortly after his oldest brother was elected President, decided that he would run for the highest office in the land. He did it to some extent because it was expected of him. Politics was a calling within the ranks of the many cousins, uncles, aunts, brothers and sisters who were part of the most prominent Irish family not just in the United States, but in the entire world. As a sitting senator whose brothers were assassinated while holding the offices of president and senator, he knew his party's nomination was all but certain. Yet winning the nomination was one thing while winning the general election quite another. There was also the realization that deep currents of hatred had taken the lives of his two brothers and there was little to suggest that it had disappeared in just a few short years.

Irish politicians and Italian criminals had much in common, the most obvious of which was their religion and the manner in which they practiced it, embraced it and at times corrupted it for their own evil purposes. And their church—The Church of Rome—played a host of roles in dealing with the "Cops and the Wops," as the Irish-Italian relationship was often referred to by many people, including some Roman Catholic priests. The Irish and Italians were both organized along male dominated lines, which permitted them to attend Church on Sundays; behave dishonestly and at times criminally during the week; heap affection upon their wives and children; and keep one or more women for their extra-curricular activities. Priests, monsignors, bishops and even cardinals were aware of it and some of them were deeply involved in what some observers referred to as debauchery. The Italian-Irish-Church *triangle of hypocrisy* was held together by a desire for power. But strangely, there were also a few good men, especially some priests, who were motivated by a simple desire for the greater good. Thinking *the triangle* had also done much that was of value, they did their best to hold it together. Archbishop Calogero Ferraro was one such priest.

A Sicilian by birth, Archbishop Ferraro was appointed by the Pope as the Vatican's ambassador to the United Nations with the title of Apostolic Nuncio. Although he was technically one level below a cardinal, as the Pope's hand-picked representative to the United Nations his words and opinions could not be ignored, not even by a Cardinal. Since he resided in New York City he had frequent contacts with the nation's largest Italian American communities in the City and to the south in New Jersey and Pennsylvania. Yet dealing with the Italian American community was a challenge, even for a Sicilian who was also a priest. There was also a substantial Irish American population in the City, but the center of Irish influence was to the north in the Boston area where the Irish political machine had produced the country's first Catholic president as well as several senators, governors and a number of ambassadors. The Archbishop knew the slain President's family well and had played a "behind the pulpit" role in support of his election.

The Irish had their Saint Patrick's Day celebration that was something of a national holiday extending well beyond the Irish American community. Even Protestants took part in activities including parades and performances which rarely failed to conclude with widespread public drunkenness. The Italians, who were outnumbered by the Irish two to one in the United States, had numerous smaller festivals although Columbus Day celebrations had special meaning for them. The Archbishop's calendar included many ethnic gatherings, great and small, including one in North Slope, Pennsylvania for a Saint Maro festival sponsored by the church his good friend, Monsignor Lessari, had presided over. There he would drink wine, smoke Cuban cigars and play cards with the Monsignor and other Italian men.

The Monsignor's murder troubled him deeply and it left him in a quandary. Why was he killed? Were his ties to Italian crime families the reason for his death? In the absence of the Monsignor, who could he turn to when he needed to influence powerful Italian Americans, many of whom were in some way connected to organized crime?

Although he was a worldly man, the Archbishop was a decent person to his very core, willing to help anyone in need. To help the many, however, he needed to deal with and satisfy the rich and powerful including those who were dirty. It was a dilemma he shared with Monsignor Lessari and they often spoked of it. Ironically, the Monsignor was his backdoor conduit to the most powerful Italian criminals, many of whom were located just a short distance from his office at the United Nations building in New York City. Surprisingly, for decades a few families from the hard coal region of Pennsylvania had an unbreakable alliance with one New York City crime family. Through that family they cooperated with other Italian criminal elements of the City. The Monsignor and the Archbishop understood the workings of criminals and politicians. They used it to help elect the assassinated President, and they would have used it again to help the next brother seek that office, had he not also been assassinated.

Never before had Tony Martino been summoned to New York City by the head of the family. All his previous communications with Cosmo DeGalanti were short verbal messages by telephone or delivered by an associate of the family who was passing through Lock Haven, Pennsylvania. The messages were always coded, so it would have been very difficult for anyone to get their true meaning, even if they were intercepted by the police. Telephone conversations were always pay-telephone to pay-telephone and the locations of the telephones were always *setup* at the last minute by others, making it nearly impossible for their short conversations to be wire tapped. Tony and Cosmo DeGalanti were both secretive and careful, which is why neither of them had ever been convicted of a crime.

Cosmo DeGalanti and his son Neil were seated at a small round table on the ninth floor of a still incomplete apartment building when Tony arrived. Construction workers were told by their union representatives to stay out of the area for two hours. After the usual greeting, hand shake and kiss on the left cheek, they began. How to stop the Senator from becoming President of the United States was the only issue.

"The Senator must not become President!" Tony and Neil knew how he felt and Tony was willing to do whatever it took to satisfy the old man. But Neil was concerned that Tony would simply kill the Senator thereby setting off a firestorm destroying everything the family had built over the years. He had convinced his father to call Tony in before it was too late. Surely, he believed, killing the Senator had to be totally removed from any strategy Tony and his father were considering. "I know that's what you want Tony, but killing the Senator will result in the destruction of everything we do," Neil said. Tony sat silently, which was completely out of character for him, although Neil knew Tony could turn inward and plot his own course of action while ignoring everything around him.

Neil's father replied, "Doing nothing will also do us great harm, it may even destroy us. Know this—they are no better than us. If they eliminate us their friends will take our place. Then they'd win every election and control every judge. Before long the whole country would be theirs."

"Never! Sure, winning the president's office would make them stronger, but not strong enough to take over." Neil looked at Tony hoping for support, but didn't receive it. The heated discussion between Neil and his father continued for some time while Tony continued his silence, which was beginning to unnerve Neil.

The old man, Cosmo DeGalanti, replied with great certainty.

"They'll bring in people from Ireland, the ones fighting the British in their northern area; they'll line up the criminals from Boston, the ones the FBI protects; and they'll also get help from the crazy Irish right here in New York City."

"The Westies? We have a truce with them that helps all of us. Why would they end that?"

"Stupido!" His father replied, "The Westies would replace us and then they would control the whole city—OUR CITY!"

Neil knew his father was right about one thing. The Westies from New York City and Irish criminals from the Boston area, if combined with violent elements imported from Ireland, would create a lethal combination. The Irish Republican Army, the IRA, had waged a vicious war against the British military in Northern Ireland for years with surprising success. And they had strong connections in the Boston area where they often raised money in Irish communities which they used to feed their war efforts. Although it was illegal, they did it openly. In addition to all of that, the FBI cooperated with the Irish mob in Boston. Their pro-Irish and anti-Italian biases were so deep that they allowed low level Italian criminals to be convicted for murders they didn't commit. Then they sat on evidence they knew would exonerate these men as they rotted in prison for years. The old man was right and Neil now recognized it. If the Senator was elected President, the Italian crime families would face an all-out war they could not possibly win, with the IRA, the Westies, the Boston mob, the FBI and the rest of the federal government all aligned against them. Yet killing the Senator could produce the same results.

"Hey, stupido," Tony said with a smile before he added, "Short of killing the Senator, what can we do?"

"I don't know ... just don't kill the Senator or anyone from his family or staff."

"Nah," the old man said. "That's too much ... Tony," he spoke softly for he had figured it out. "kill only lesser men, even if from his family or staff—only the lesser men who aren't important!"

Neil was surprised and somewhat relieved. "Lesser men, yes lesser men. Not the Senator; not anyone in his immediate family; and not his key staff members."

The old man was elated. His son and Tony Martino, who meant much to him, would work together to stop the Irish menace. And if killing needed to be done, Tony would kill only lesser men.

The election was more than a year off, yet the Irish, the Italians and the Church of Rome needed to prepare. Archbishop Ferraro wanted a Roman Catholic President, but he also wanted peace between the two largest Roman Catholic communities in the country. In the past, he would simply express his wishes and concerns to Monsignor Lessari and in a short time the appropriate parties would be informed. The Monsignor's murder changed things, but before long he identified a suitable substitute—Frank Martino, the father of Tony. He was a devout Roman Catholic and widely respected by the hard coal region's Italian population. He was also head of one of the region's two crime families.

Neither the Italians nor the Irish could afford to offend the Archbishop, for fear of losing support from the highest levels of the Church. Their spiritual connections to the Church were deep, and in strange and complex ways their family, community and emotional ties to the Church went back not just for decades, but for generations. To offend the Archbishop, who was also the Pope's hand-picked representative to the United Nations, was simply unthinkable. Yet the Irish were aware that he was not only Italian, he was Sicilian!

The Archbishop's request was surprisingly simple. He asked that they come together and attempt to put past differences behind them. Furthermore, he indicated his availability to serve as a mediator if their efforts failed. He made it clear that he favored neither party, but in his heart, he hoped for another Roman Catholic to be elected President of the United States.

Suddenly the Irish were elated—the Pope's representative wanted the Senator to become President!

There was no shortage of restaurants in New York City where police, firemen, politicians and criminals gathered and respected the neutrality of eating fine food, and drinking good wine and whiskey.

Tony, Neil DeGalanti and Father Callahan arrived first and positioned themselves at the back of the restaurant, well away from the bar. Tony felt that having a priest, especially an Irish priest, on their side was a good play. He also knew that the good Father was no ordinary priest, having served as a combat officer during the Korean War before he was ordained. Although Father Callahan was once a close friend of Tony's, their friendship had ended months before when he was caught cheating at poker and beaten for his dishonesty. Nevertheless, he owed Tony a sizeable amount of money and depended on him to maintain his lavish lifestyle. He was fond of good food and wine, not to mention his prostitute girlfriend.

The Senator's group arrived a short time later. Neil immediately recognized two of them for the wrong reasons. The Senator's Cousin was his top political advisor and had made national news for beating his wife during a drunken rampage. She forgave him, but not before the papers spread his picture and hers across numerous editions. Other family members of the Senator's had some degree of celebrity status often for their womanizing and drunken episodes, so the Senator and his staff did what they always did—shrug their shoulders and wait for time to pass. Neil ignored the extended hand from the Senator's Cousin and pointing at the man to his right said, "He shouldn't be here, he's a Westie!" It was a bad start and the Cousin wasn't sure why.

The Westie, a tall scruffy young man added to the unease by shouting back at Neil, "So what? You brought a goddamn priest and you're too fucken cheap to set up any drinks!"

The Cousin wanted things to go smoothly so he asked everyone to sit. They did and Tony looked across the table at the third member of the opposition and asked where he was from. "North Ireland," he replied with a brogue thick enough that it could be cut with an Italian stiletto. There was little doubt he was IRA.

Neil and the Senator's Cousin began with a low-key discussion about the path the assassinated President had taken to the nation's highest office, paying attention to the contributions made by Italian criminal organizations and their many friends in Hollywood, labor unions, the Church and in politics.

When the waitress brought the drinks, the Westie pulled her close to him and grabbed hold of her left breast. She slapped him and he released her with a vulgar comment.

"That's no way to treat a woman!" Father Callahan spoke through clenched teeth.

"How would you know; your kind only fools around with altar boys and nuns?"

The exchange brought a moment of exasperated silence after which the two primary spokesmen continued their discussion. They were both especially interested in labor unions. The Italians were interested in the money, access to goods and pure muscle the unions could provide to their extensive enterprises, especially in the City. The Irish wanted the same thing although their greatest interest was in the votes they could produce, sometimes illegally. Not wanting to miss out on a golden opportunity, the Senator's Cousin said, "I also expect a taste of the wealth to move our way."

Neil and Tony were encouraged by that remark believing, to some extent, in "honor among thieves." Referring to the deal the Westies made with Italian criminals in New York City, the Westie inserted, "And we want a cut of any action, just like the deal the Wops gave us right here."

The discussion went on nearly two more hours before the Westie spoke up again. "Isn't it time to eat something? This place should have good steaks and half decent *It al e ann oh* food."

In spite of the Westie's behavior, the discussions had been more productive than either side expected. Yet there was still the issue of trust, to which Father Callahan offered, "In ancient times potential adversaries would exchange hostages as a way of maintaining peace and cooperation; even the Romans and Greeks did it."

"Great, we'll take you, and set you up in a church with a supply of altar boys," was the response from directly across the table.

The food was served—Italian for the Irish and steaks for the other three. Tony decided against using the knife provided by the restaurant, relying instead on the dagger attached to his belt. "There are many ways of building trust," he said, while staring intently into the green eyes of the IRA member sitting directly across from him. Although they had rarely spoken, it was clear from their body language that he and Tony were in agreement about most of the issues the two sides had discussed. They could feel or sense it in each other, perhaps because both their souls had been stained with the blood of other men.

The conversation slowed as the men ate. Yet once again Tony repeated, "There are many ways of building trust." This time he stared at the Senator's Cousin and positioned the dagger between them, with the handle away from himself, as if he were handing it to him.

The Cousin put his hand on Tony's knife and for a time turned inward. After what seemed like a long time he slowly moved the knife to his left. In a soft voice, almost a whisper, he said, "Get rid of him," to the man the IRA knew as Johnny Boy.

He moved quickly, like a large cat, and in one motion placed a table napkin in the Westie's mouth and the dagger into his back. As if it had been rehearsed, Father Callahan grabbed the right arm of the victim and in a loud voice shouted, "You've had too much to drink my son; let me help you." They were well away from the bar area where most of the customers were gathered and it wasn't uncommon for friends to help a drunken comrade.

Johnny Boy and the good Father made it look easy as they moved the Westie to the rear door while talking good naturally about *their friend's* drinking habits. Once outside they disposed of the body in a garbage dumpster. It wouldn't be the first time the garbage collection on the edge of Westie territory included a body.

Cosmo DeGalanti was surprised when he learned what had transpired during the Italian-Irish *sit down*. He knew, however, that politics could produce complex and unexpected alliances. Although he was still suspicious of the Irish, he didn't want to dismiss what could be a profitable future business endeavor. He was also amused when he discovered that an Irish Roman Catholic priest had participated in the killing of a Westie.

By 1950 the Irish criminals had been driven from most of New York City by their Italian rivals and Jewish allies. The Dagos had defeated the

Micks where it counted—the most important commercial center in the world, where money flowed like water and influence was bought and sold, as were vast quantities of illegal drugs and untaxed cigarettes. Yet there remained one small bastion within New York City where Irish criminality controlled the streets and the people remained loyal to them—Hell's Kitchen!

Although there were at least 100 soldiers in the Italian crime families for every member of the Hell's Kitchen Irish mob, the Irish murdered more brutally, often following the killings with gruesome body dismemberment orgies. The identity of the killers was in many cases widely known, yet the Westies were so feared that convictions were rare. After one well documented murder, the killer told the father he murdered his son and promised to do the same to him and other members of his family if they cooperated with the police. They didn't. Gruesome killings by the Irish mob resulted in a public outcry during the 1970s that was so strong the Italian crime families feared the resulting criminal investigations could harm them. Far more pragmatic and organized than their Irish counterparts, the Italians did the unthinkable. The Italians struck a deal with the Irish that would ultimately benefit both sides. The Irish mob received cooperation from the Italians that translated into enormous amounts of money and some degree of respectability. In exchange, the Irish reduced their violence and murdered only in extreme situations and only when sanctioned by the Italians.

SAINTS AND SINNERS

———◆———

A Jewish attorney from Philadelphia who worked for the mob and eventually ended up in trouble with the police, Benjamin Sherman was a cliché. In the midst of a brutal divorce from his attorney-wife, she falsely accused him of raping her and the police were happy to go after him. Outraged, he threw a punch and that ended his legal career. He was arrested, convicted and disbarred.

Benjamin should have known better. The daughter he had with his secretary couldn't remain a secret from his wife forever. Still, she was twelve when his wife found out. Divorce can be messy and brutal, and his wife used every dirty trick she could think of against him. When she charged him with rape, the police were delighted to put the screws to an attorney who had beaten them in court many times. When it was all said and done, Benjamin had served thirty days in jail, no longer had a license to practice law and had sole custody of his daughter Maggie. Once he could no longer support the secretary she dropped him and their daughter. Nevertheless, he believed he was better off. Relationships with two women he never loved had come to an end, replaced with the unconditional love that a father and his daughter could openly express for the first time.

Unlike most Jewish men, Benjamin loved outdoor activities, especially fishing and hunting. Years before his divorce, when the opportunity presented itself, he purchased a deer camp on a tract of land on the southern edge of Dead Indian Swamp, adjoining the much larger property that Tony Martino owned. With the Philadelphia legal establishment firmly against him, Benjamin knew his ex-wife would get most of their assets. He grudgingly accepted her divorce settlement offer—he got the deer camp and she got everything else. Fortunately, he had salted away some cash as a hedge against the unforeseen. It was a tactic his mob clients used that often resulted in *cash off the books* payments for his services. Things would be financially tough, but not nearly as bad as it would seem.

The deed for the land his hunting camp was located on presented a problem which Benjamin quickly recognized when he bought it. It was also the reason the purchase price was so low. The land was surrounded on three sides by Tony Martino's property, and on the fourth side by a steep drop-off that was impossible to ascend with a road, no matter how much money Benjamin would be willing to spend. However, he bought the deer camp knowing the previous owner had received written permission to cross Martino's land, and that was unlikely to change. Besides, Benjamin reasoned, his previous work for Italian mob figures in the Philly area would put him in good standing with Tony Martino.

Back when he regularly attended synagogue, Benjamin once quipped, "If you're unlucky, it's a good thing to remember your Jewish roots." Benjamin often compared the histories of Italians and Jews and was well aware of the times they fought and others when they cooperated. Jewish lawyers were greatly respected by Italian criminals and some were corrupted by the association. Benjamin was, yet he had no regrets. He loved the competition that placed him between his clients and the vast array of resources that government agencies could use to attack them. Very often the government violated the very rules they were expected to defend, and he didn't care about doing the same. The Pennsylvania Crime Commission destroyed reputations of many people with little regard for the truth or rights protected by the Constitution. Some police officers planted evidence and grand jury testimony was often leaked by prosecutors in violation of the law and all codes of ethics the legal profession was expected to follow. If a District Attorney believed someone was guilty but couldn't prove it in court, damaging grand jury testimony was leaked to the press. "The accused," the subject of the grand jury investigation, was then forced to defend himself in the "court of public opinion." In response, Benjamin "gamed the system" on behalf of his clients. He had a stable of witnesses who could be "coached" into providing testimony that supported his clients. More importantly, he had a bench of expert witnesses who could challenge even the most concrete evidence offered by the prosecution. They were called "hired guns" for good reason—they could "shoot down" or at least call into question almost any evidence. Even eye witness accounts could be challenged by introducing medical testimony regarding a witness's visual and hearing acuity. And although Benjamin fit in nicely with Tony's circle of friends, he wasn't one of his closest associates—only violent criminals and blood relatives were allowed into that darkness.

The Wednesday night poker game had become more than famous; it was slowly becoming legendary. A priest was once beaten for cheating at cards. Tony's cousin was believed murdered while the game was in progress and participants in the game suddenly became involved in the drama that followed. Seemingly in response, a fire bombing took place a short time later killing two courthouse employees and their children. All of that and for a price a beautiful woman would be very accommodating—although that was supposed to be a tightly held secret.

Father Callahan was delighted to return to the game. He had assisted in the killing of a Westie so Tony rewarded him by forgiving the large amount of money the Priest owed him.

It would be an interesting night of card playing. Tony, George, Father Callahan, Benjamin Sherman and Sheriff Marsit playing cards seemed like a setup for a joke—*An Italian criminal, his priest, a cop, a newspaper reporter and a disbarred attorney walked into a bar and ...* Yet, they were a sinister lot. Paula Mary had returned to her previous role of *hostess* for the group and she was well aware of how it had evolved in just a short time. She was especially concerned that something might be said which she shouldn't hear. And the men did talk, always in carefully measured tones so as not to reveal too much. Yet there needed to be some level of openness so that relationships could be maintained and strengthened.

"Hey, Father Callahan," George said, in his usual booming voice. "I heard you and Tony are switching sides. Supporting that Irish Senator makes sense for you, an Irish priest, but how did you corrupt Tony into supporting him?"

"I can talk for myself ... Keep your options open. I live by that. It just seemed to me that the Senator won't make the mistakes his brothers made."

"You mean going after Italian crooks?"

"Hell no, I mean the goddamn Vietnam War and that Cuban mess! The President and his brother did things that led to tens of thousands of men dying in Vietnam, and with Cuba they nearly started a fucking nuclear war."

Tony said it with conviction and George seemed to agree with him. "You must think he can't be stopped; he'll get the presidency no matter what, so join him. I'm just surprised that you think he'll be fair with Italians like yourself." George was always looking for a news story although he still hadn't figured out how to write an article about ethnic influences in presidential politics.

The game continued for several hours. Around 1 AM the phone rang and a sigh went up from the group. "A call at this time of night; it can't be good," Sheriff Marsit said, while shaking his head.

George took the call and almost immediately said, "Ben, call your daughter."

The game continued as Benjamin went off to the side and called his daughter. Then he made a second call.

Laughing and shaking his head in disbelief, Benjamin said, "You guys won't believe it. There's a warrant out for Tony's arrest!"

"Now what the fuck did I do?"

"Don't worry Tony; this isn't going anywhere. The charge against you is for beating the hell out of that guy from the Crime Commission. They said it happened around 9 PM. Hell, that's just four hours ago, and you were here with us!"

"Oh my God," George bellowed with disbelief and amusement in his voice.

"Yeah, and there's more. Your tall blonde girlfriend helped you. She held him and his wife at gun point while you pistol whipped him."

Even Father Callahan was amused. "Where do you hide your girlfriend, Tony?"

"Do you believe this?" George said to himself, as he made a phone call. He gave the information to the night editor and told him to call Carol so she could "punch up" the text.

"Hold on," the Sheriff inserted. "You don't know enough to run with that story. This might all be a hoax."

"I assure you," Benjamin replied, "this is not a hoax! My source has a direct line to the Philly Police."

"I present the news fairly and those assholes at the Pennsylvania Crime Commission report that I'm a member of a crime family. Nazi bastards, I'll get them!"

That Saturday there was a small wedding ceremony in the yard outside the Martino home. It was a perfect day and all those gathered for the event could look down from the top of the mountain into the scenic valley below.

George, Benjamin and a handful of Martino family members were in attendance. Sheriff Marsit didn't know about the wedding, although Tony did consider inviting him. Father Callahan was delighted to unite the happy couple. Joey Martino and Samantha concealed their injuries very well for the most important day of their lives. Tony was the best man and Melissa the maid of honor. With a huge smile on his face, George told Tony, "It is amazing how much you and your cousin Joey look alike."

Just a few weeks earlier, Joey and Samantha had survived the attack against them that was staged by friends of Judge Archer. They had decided to remain missing, knowing it would add an element of uncertainty to the ongoing police investigations. They were *missing in action and presumed dead,* and they liked it that way. It would also make it easier to one day deal with Judge Archer's friends. Joey planned on killing three of them, when the time was right.

COOPERATION

———◆———

The war in Northern Ireland began many years before he was born and Johnny Boy believed it would continue for some time after his death. Officially, the United States government supported the British efforts to suppress the uprising, which was usually referred to as *The Troubles*. Yet even many non-Catholics in the United States were sympathetic with the plight of the Catholic minority in Northern Ireland. And among Catholics, especially Irish Catholics, the support was solid. No segment of the American population supported what was increasingly seen as a foreign government occupation of Northern Ireland, yet the American government still supported the British.

Johnny grew up during The Troubles initially throwing bricks at British soldiers and later firing a rifle at them. And he eventually became smart and deadly. It was fairly easy to pass through the border from Catholic Ireland to British owned Protestant Northern Ireland. And his passage to England meant little more than standing in line to buy a ticket for a boat ride to London. He had killed British soldiers with a rifle and three members of the Protestant paramilitary force that supported them before making his way to London. He was well trained and motivated, so it didn't take him very long. He planted a bomb in a pub near the historic Houses of Parliament. More than twenty died and although he was never identified, he became a hero to those opposing the British. Irish Catholics considered IRA members to be heroes yet the identities of most of them were never known. For good reason—being identified often meant death or being tortured at the hands of the British military or one of the police or paramilitary groups that were allied with them.

Johnny had a difficult life fighting a war he believed could never be won. But then the Irish American Senator visited Northern Ireland and was outraged at what he saw. He spoke publicly about The Troubles in Northern Ireland and said it was Britain's Vietnam. He then demanded that all British troops withdraw from the Irish island; called for a single united Ireland; and in the most incendiary way said all Protestants should leave Ireland and go back to Britain!

His words were seen as a *call to action* by the IRA and some Irish Catholics in America. From that point on Johnny and the IRA would have done anything to help him; even give their very lives in support of him. It was inevitable. When Johnny discovered that the Senator was interested in running for President of the United States, he committed himself to the election effort. Clearly the Senator, if elected president, would try to free Northern Ireland from British control. At the very least, he would make it very difficult for the British government to portray itself as a true democracy on the world stage.

The FBI was in a difficult position. It was well known that most agents in the Boston FBI office openly supported the Senator; obviously in conflict with the long-standing FBI policy and practice of staying out of politics. Johnny didn't know any of this and it didn't matter. When the Senator's Cousin gave him access to information provided by the FBI, Johnny knew he needed to act. How could he ignore a possible threat against the Senator's life? Yet what should he do—kill Italian criminals who may have done nothing more than engage in barroom bravado? He needed to move carefully, and he needed help from Tony.

Tony Martino and Johnny Boy had been moving in different circles with the same goal in mind. At least it seemed that way. Tony was quietly making the rounds with union bosses in Pennsylvania and New Jersey asking them to give the Senator support after he announced his intention to run for President. It wasn't difficult to convince them. Trying to convince those connected with the Italian mob was far more difficult. They believed they had been treated unfairly by the Senator's two brothers, both of whom had been assassinated. And they weren't inclined to forget that. The best he could hope for was that they would neither support nor oppose the Senator in his attempt to become president. He would need to work on them just to achieve that.

Johnny traveled in Irish American circles largely to raise money for the IRA. When it came to the Senator, the Irish in the United States didn't need convincing; they would strongly support him. And although it was illegal to openly collect money for the IRA, Johnny was always careful to indicate the funds would be used only to help families harmed by The Troubles. People who gave money politely listened to Johnny's pitch, but they knew most of the money would be going into the IRA's war chest.

If the threat against the Senator was legitimate, Johnny knew that Tony was the only one who could help him eliminate it. It would also be a way to test Tony's resolve and commitment to the Senator's effort. Johnny traveled to Lock Haven, Pennsylvania and spoke to Tony face-to-face.

Tony received him warmly until Johnny told him the purpose of his visit. "Two of your people are planning to kill the Senator!"

"My people?"

"Italians in New Jersey, across the river from New York City. They're union bosses in trucking, so they're part of your group. Do we call them mobsters?"

With a laugh, "Mobsters would be about right."

"I believe it's your responsibility to take care of this. Right?"

"Take care of it … you mean talk to them?"

"I think something more forceful would be in order."

Tony was still smiling, but not convinced. "Where in the hell did you get this information?"

"The FBI passed the information on to the Senator's Cousin. He gave it to me and told me to eliminate the threat, and do it quickly."

"The FBI! So why don't they just arrest the two guys?"

"For what? Can you be arrested in the United States for planning a murder?"

"Planning to murder a Senator—Hell yes!"

"Maybe they don't have solid evidence."

"Well the evidence they have … how did the FBI get it?"

"Does it matter?"

"Sure it matters. Killing two mobsters, as you call them, isn't a minor issue. We gotta be sure about it. How does the FBI know; and are there only two men involved?"

Johnny was thinking about his next step when Tony said, "If we're going to start killing people at the request of the Senator's Cousin, it better be nailed down tight right from the beginning."

He didn't trust the telephones knowing they could be tapped, so Johnny traveled to Boston to speak face-to-face with the Senator's Cousin. He returned two days later and told Tony what he had discovered. After the FBI had learned from an informant that the two men were discussing ways to kill the Senator, they wired tapped all the telephones the men used and planted listening devices in their offices and homes. Their conversations convinced the FBI that they had the Senator in their sights. Yet their conversations weren't sufficiently specific, so the FBI believed it didn't have enough evidence to arrest them and make it stick.

Tony needed time to figure it all out. He was especially concerned about the informant, something he didn't share with Johnny.

Johnny was happy to stay at Tony's home as they slowly developed a plan. Because of The Troubles in his homeland, it had been years since he enjoyed the peace and security of a normal home. Tony's family was gracious to him and when it came to Melissa's sister Carol—like many men, he was attracted to her.

Johnny was in Lock Haven for only a few days and had already met most of Tony's friends. He was introduced to Paula Mary but didn't know about the services she provided during the Wednesday night poker game Tony and his friends enjoyed. He never had a long-term relationship with a woman, which was unusual for a man in his early thirties. It was a shortcoming he recognized and had been willing to accept in exchange for a life as a fighter in the war against the British in Ireland. But meeting Carol and Paula Mary produced a stirring that reached to his soul. And he wouldn't have been inclined to harshly judge either of them for their morally questionable relationships with men.

It was Tuesday and Johnny enjoyed the three days he had spent with Tony and his family. That morning the story of a gangland killing in New Jersey exploded across the news. Three men who were believed to be part of organized crime had been murdered and their bodies were dumped in a landfill. Johnny didn't know what to make of it. Tony did. A telephone call a short time later confirmed it. George called Tony to ask his opinion about something he had heard from a New Jersey journalist. "I've been told one of the three dead men was an FBI informant."

"How would anyone know that?"

"I don't know if they're certain of it. Either this guy got a leak from the FBI or he figured it out for himself. He works for a paper in New Jersey, so he probably has contacts with the FBI and the Jersey mob. I just want to know your take on it. Would the mob kill three men just to get one informant?"

"Well I'm not an expert on the mob," Tony said with a laugh, knowing his telephone was probably tapped. "It seems like a reasonable thing to do. Hell, one traitor on the inside could destroy the whole organization."

Johnny was listening in on the conversation and had figured it out. He had told Tony about the informant and he passed the word up the line. His anger with Tony, however, was tempered by the realization that the IRA had also killed suspected informants. And more than once it was discovered later that the wrong person was murdered. Yet killing three men just to be sure you got rid of the informant—Johnny wasn't sure what to make of it.

Seeing the concern on Johnny's face, Tony surprised him by saying, "This is a good, because it cleans things up. Now we can focus on getting rid of the two men you're concerned about." Johnny wasn't entirely happy with killing three men to eliminate the FBI informant, but he was a pragmatist. The killings were in the past and his goal was to protect the Senator.

The next night, Wednesday night, the poker game took place as usual. Tony had delayed traveling to New Jersey to take care of the two union officials so that Johnny could participate in the game and connect on a man-to-man basis with his inner circle. The election was still more than a year off and the Senator hadn't even announced his intention to run for the office of president. Yet if Tony intended to help the Senator, Johnny and his inner circle would of necessity be involved. If, however, the opposite occurred—events indicated the Senator should be stopped—he would still need his inner circle. Yet opposing the Senator would mean dealing with Johnny.

Experience had demonstrated that things could get out of control very quickly at the poker game. Sheriff Marsit wasn't sure what to make of Johnny, so initially he didn't ask any questions. George, however, was always the newsman looking for a story. A man from Northern Ireland in the United States helping a Senator was certainly interesting even if he didn't look below the surface. "Tell me Johnny, did you ever see any violence over there during The Troubles?"

After a brief pause, "A bit, but I tried to stay clear. It's too messy. There's too many sides. And if you look at one of the Queen's soldiers the wrong way, you could end up in prison. And from there … well there are stories of torture and beatings. That's what you hear. Can't tell if it's true, because some men, the British said they were IRA, were taken from their homes and locked up. No trial, just locked up for years."

"I don't believe it," Sheriff Marsit said, and added, "The British wouldn't do that."

Support for Johnny came from Father Callahan. "You've never been in combat, in an actual war. Men do things they would never do during peace time." The good Father was recalling things he did in combat during the Korean War.

A few hours of drinking and card playing went by, and the conversation became more aggressive. Ben Sherman asked the Sheriff, "Do you think that guy on the Crime Commission will ever return Tony's gold coin—the one he took from the grave of Tony's wife?"

The Sheriff was still a police officer although he realized that he had willingly associated with Tony for several years and benefited from it. "Let's be fair about it. Tony can't be sure he's the one who took the coin.

Someone took it, I'm sure Tony and his son are right about that. I just have some doubts that someone who was once a State Cop would do it."

"Did you at least approach the guy about returning the coin?"

"Now Tony, think about it. That's like asking a man, 'When's the last time you beat your wife?' I can't ask him about the coin; it would seem like I'm accusing him."

"A police officer stealing a gold coin? Sounds like Northern Ireland. I know men, including police officers, who have been shot for doing less. Something like that would eat at me."

"Listen Johnny," the Sheriff replied, "this ain't Ireland. We don't kill a police officer because he might have done something wrong. And speaking of accusing somebody about a crime ... Tony, didn't you have the Commissioner beaten?"

"You must be drunk—you have no problem accusing me of a crime, but not that guy from the Crime Commission." Tony was laughing, the Sheriff wasn't.

The game ended around 3 AM. Johnny offered to walk Paula Mary home but she declined his offer. She left instead with Father Callahan.

Tony and Johnny drove to New Jersey expecting to observe the two men who needed killing—men the FBI believed were conspiring to kill the Senator. They should have realized it wouldn't be easy. FBI agents and New Jersey State Police were everywhere. Killing three men, one of whom was an FBI informant, resulted in an extraordinary response. In addition, the news people were also about scratching for information. Seeing it first hand, Tony believed it would be best to pull back and do it at a later date. Getting close enough to kill two men with a knife or a gun, while avoiding the police and the press, seemed like an impossible task. But Johnny knew exactly how to do it. At least how to kill one of the men with a remote-controlled bomb. Building and safely detonating one was something he learned to do in Ireland; all he needed were supplies and a little time.

After returning to North Slope, only two hours away, Tony and Johnny went to the anthracite mining area where explosives were easily found in the garage his cousin Joey owned. Finding blasting caps and dynamite sticks was easy. The remote control was the difficult part. Tony removed it from the garage door opener that was used by Joey at his home. Tony asked about range and Johnny smiled saying, "I've done it before. Just enlarge the antenna on the receiving end and build up the output on the transmitter. It only needs to work once, so if we over power the whole transmitter-receiver it won't matter."

"No, it better work twice ... we'll need to test the damn thing before we actually use it."

They tried it out, without explosives attached, and the remote signal was received at a distance of one-thousand meters. Tony was impressed; Johnny could kill far more elegantly than he ever could.

It was after midnight when they returned to the building that housed the union office where the two men worked. The area was surrounded by warehouses and there wasn't anyone around. An old pickup truck was near the entrance the men would use to enter the building. The truck wasn't locked so they took off the hand brake and moved it close to the entrance. Dynamite, blasting cap and receiver had been wrapped into a lethal package that Johnny positioned on the passenger side of the truck before locking the doors. The scene was set.

Not wanting to be noticed, they waited in the car. Johnny had covered the license plate with dirt so the number couldn't be seen. He had also covered the car in coal dirt while they were in Pennsylvania, telling Tony, "The Devil is in the details."

Truckers start early. Shortly after sunrise things began to stir so they left the car and walked slowly around the area trying to blend in. Truckers tend to mind their own business so they weren't noticed. "This isn't an exact science," Johnny told Tony. "I'm not sure how big the blast will be; not even sure it'll work. But as I told you before, it only needs to work once."

They were located about 500 meters away, a bit over a quarter of a mile, but they had a clear view of the truck, although at that distance they couldn't make out faces. They knew the cars both men drove so they figured to use the arrival of either car as the signal to detonate.

Cars were beginning to show up and around 8 AM a car belonging to one of the intended victims pulled up. Johnny didn't trust Tony with his work, so he held the transmitter in his hands. The car had parked directly behind the truck. A few seconds passed before someone exited the car on the passenger side. Johnny hesitated, but he knew someone needed to die. The man took two steps, Johnny pushed the button and … not only did the bomb go off as expected, a second explosion from the truck's gas tank followed … and less than a second later the gas tank of the car exploded. The three explosions seemed like one. A moment later fire jumped to the building. People ran away from the blast, although a few brave souls moved toward the fire and the secondary victims located as much as one-hundred feet from the truck and car.

Tony entered their car expecting to speed off. "Not yet," Johnny yelled, as he stood fixated by what they had done. Others stood nearby not knowing how to react. Johnny knew it was unwise to leave too quickly, because it might signify prior knowledge. "Just wait," he cautioned. Before long firemen and police descended on the scene and asked people to leave the area. The fire was still roaring.

Johnny entered the car and said, "Now would be a good time to leave." His voice was calm.

It took several days for the final figures to come in. One of the two men they were targeting had been killed, as was his son. He had driven his father to work and planned on using the car the rest of the day. An FBI agent was in a car across the street and was also killed. Twenty others were seriously injured.

The FBI assumed it was a continuation of mob violence that had taken the lives of three men just ten days earlier. The investigation went on for weeks. One technician on the FBI payroll indicated the bomb's construction was remarkably similar to those used by the IRA in Northern Ireland.

FROM THE PAST

The Senator was shocked and deeply troubled by the six killings. When he told his Cousin about the threat against him, which he had been made aware of by the FBI, he realized that there could be a reaction by the people who wanted him to be elected. He didn't specifically authorize it, but he knew it might be necessary to kill one man, and he was prepared to live with that. If it became public, he might be able to explain one killing as a tragic mistake. If that failed, he would try to justified it as an act of self-defense made on his behalf by a misguided supporter, yet neither approach would have been easy. He also didn't understand what had happened to the FBI informant and he was especially concerned that the violence wasn't over.

Cosmo DeGalanti, the undisputed head of Tony's crime family, was surprised by the last three of the six killings. He couldn't tolerate an FBI informant anywhere within Italian organized crime circles, so he took no chances and had three men killed knowing one of the three was the informer. It wasn't neat, but it was effective, and the other crime families supported the action. The other murders, however, were not approved by him. When he learned that Tony was involved and it was done to protect the Senator, he saw an opportunity. If necessary, he could now connect the Senator to a number of killings, including an FBI agent and a member of the Westies. He believed the Senator had found his way into the same darkness where he lived, which meant the Senator could never turn on the mob the way his two brothers had. If elected, the

Senator would be unlikely to object too forcefully if the crime families expanded their operations. He also knew that the rash of killings would result in an aggressive investigation by the FBI.

The FBI was looking under every rock and was willing to use questionable practices to solve the increasing number of murders that had been dropped on their doorstep, especially the killing of an FBI agent. Tony wasn't a prime suspect; he was just one of many Italians the FBI believed to be a criminal. Yet they couldn't connect him in any way to a specific crime. However, one FBI agent, Henry Johns, took a keen interest in Tony and was shocked at what he soon learned. He was present when Tony was questioned by the Pennsylvania State Police in the Clinton County Courthouse and left there with an uneasy feeling about him. Further examination of Tony's past produced some interesting information. A significant number of men who came in contact with him died under suspicious circumstances; several who know him were murdered; and one close friend simply vanished. Digging deeply into his record it was clear Martino had been violent in the past although not enough so that he could be arrested. One violent encounter had taken place while he was in high school and resulted in deep hatred between Tony's family and friends, and a powerful hard coal region family whose two sons had physically harmed Sandy, a young woman Tony loved like a sister. Agent Johns found that to be very interesting. Then he discovered that one of the two sons who had attacked Sandy was murdered two years later while in South Carolina. Coincidence? Agent Johns didn't think so.

Further investigation into the murder revealed that the father of the man who had been murdered was himself under investigation for a host of crimes. And he wasn't Italian or in any way connected with the mob. In fact, he was known to have a deep hatred for both the Italian mob and Irish politicians. It was becoming clear to the agent that the amount of violence, hatred and corruption swirling around the hard coal region was unprecedented.

Agent Johns was with Fred White, a Pennsylvania State Trooper and Robert Stokes, a member of the Pennsylvania Crime Commission, when they questioned Tony about the murders of Judge Archer and

Monsignor Lessari. He came away from that meeting convinced that the Commission was ineffective, and understood why it was despised by both criminals and people in law enforcement. When he learned that the Commission member who was there that day was beaten by someone who apparently looked like Tony, it was easy to figure out. Tony had set it up probably using a relative who resembled him to actually administer the punishment. That way he both embarrassed the Commission when it was discovered he was wrongly accused, and at the same time he punished the Commissioner.

Believing the murder of the young man in South Carolina was probably done by Tony, or at his direction, the agent decided to investigate further.

Alfred Rheiner's ancestors had arrived in the hard coal region of Pennsylvania more than 100 years before Tony Martino's family. They acquired vast tracts of land and initially used it for lumbering and agriculture. Once hard coal was discovered in Schuylkill and Luzerne counties, they started mining it. That led to later investments in railroads and iron production. Their wealth became enormous, and soon they owned banks, salons, restaurants—they owned everything, even cities! The miners worked for them, rented houses from them, bought food from their stores and lived in their communities, commonly known as *company towns*. Decades later they evolved into what became known as *patch towns*. So complete was their control that they even owned the police, *The Coal and Iron Police,* which was established with the blessing of the Commonwealth of Pennsylvania. The Rheiners and several other families had created the equivalent of a European Principality that lasted for decades. Shifting economic, political and social forces eventually brought reform to the region, which allowed other power centers to develop. The Roman Catholic Church and Italian criminal organizations were the most notable. Yet the Rheiners, especially Alfred Rheiner, still had great power and influence throughout the region.

Agent Johns arranged for a meeting with Alfred Rheiner. It took place at a bank he owned just outside of North Slope. After a brief introduction, the Agent began. "I'd like to ask you about the murder of your son Carl."

"Why now, after five or six years? And why the FBI?

"Fair question. There's been six killings in New Jersey which are of great interest to the FBI. In addition, a priest and a judge were murdered on the same day in Pennsylvania under extraordinary circumstances. That's why we're looking at all unsolved murders that are ... well seemingly related and interesting from the point of view of ..."

"Hum, my son's death is interesting—cut the bull. This is about that bastard Tony Martino! He killed my son. I know it, and you know it."

"Well, not exactly. But if his guilt is so obvious, why didn't the police in South Carolina arrest him?"

"They had no evidence. Hell, they weren't even able to talk to him. I told them he did it and why he did it. He even told my two sons he'd one day kill both of them. And why? Because they roughed up his whore girlfriend. They didn't rape her, just pushed her around. Then he and his mobster friend, Jack Capilano, beat the hell out of my two sons."

"Why couldn't the police from South Carolina talk to him?"

"They reached him by telephone. He told them to speak to his attorney, which they did. The attorney told them to travel to Pennsylvania. He said once there, he and Martino would speak with them."

"Then what happened?"

"What happened? Nothing, absolutely nothing! They told me they had nothing to connect him to the murder so there was no point in wasting time."

All of it made sense to Agent Johns. Everything except why the father, who had great resources and greater anger, didn't act on his own. "Mr. Rheiner, you don't seem like the kind of man who would take the death of your son lightly."

He was silent for a long while before slowly saying, "I lost my sons and ..."

"Sons! I thought you had two sons and only one was murdered. I am truly sorry for your loss, but what the hell is going on?"

Once again, he was silent for a time. He wanted to explode with anger, but he also wanted help. Believing the FBI might be able to get

Tony Martino, he explained, "Years ago, before I was married, I had a relationship with a woman. We had two sons and my wife never knew about it; at least not when we first got married. It was hard, but I tried to be a father to those boys. I loved them and they loved me."

"You think he killed one of those sons?"

"No, both of them!"

The agent couldn't believe it. "Why isn't there any record of their murders?"

"Because they were never reported. Never reported because they're officially missing, I guess. There's no bodies, no evidence, nothing."

"How could that happen? When did it happen?"

"I'm not exactly sure."

"None of this makes sense."

"Not to me either. I saw the two of them as much as I could, which wasn't much. They were two very big men who loved to wander around in the wilderness, more like animals at times than men. We'd hunt and fish together and I told them about the murder of my son, their half-brother. I also told them about Martino. They became angry and told me that one day they'd even the score ... I'm almost certain they tried."

"The two of them tried and he killed both of them—is that what you're telling me?"

"Not at the same time. One day I went to see my sons and one of them was missing. His mother said he went to get some guy. I figured it was Martino ... My son never returned."

"What about the other son?"

"Less than a year later the same thing happened. I don't understand that because Martino was in Arizona at the time."

"You kept track of Martino?"

"Damn right I did. Wouldn't you?"

"Why? Unless you were planning to do something."

"I was tempted, but it wouldn't have been easy. Look what happened to my two oldest sons when they went after Martino ... but I know they weren't very smart. If I made an effort, even if I was successful, Martino's family would probably figure it out and come after me ... I have one son left and I'd like to see him live a long life."

"I'm not sure I believe you."

"It doesn't matter. Someday, someone will put a bullet in that bastard's head, but it won't be me. I just hope I don't get blamed for it."

Agent Johns was dumbfounded when he left. He carefully prepared notes of his meeting with Mr. Rheiner and included his concerns. It was circulated among the other agents who were involved in investigating what had become a series of murders starting with the Judge and Monsignor and ending with the FBI agent and the union boss. In addition to those killings, it was clear that three of Mr. Rheiner's four sons had also been murdered. The report was circulated to law enforcement agencies in Pennsylvania and New Jersey on a *need to know* basis. Special attention was given to Sheriff Marsit, Tony's friend. Agent Johns believed he wasn't involved in any of the murders and that he wouldn't protect Tony when it came to serious crimes. Smaller crimes perhaps, but not murder.

The big day was rapidly approaching. Melissa O'Donnell and Tony Martino were in the final week prior to their wedding. Melissa wanted to separate herself from Tony prior to the big day, so she moved into a motel in Lock Haven while continuing to prepare for the event. Tony remained at their mountaintop home with Olga and his two sons. He was preparing the area around their home for an outdoor wedding and reception when the Sheriff arrived. He knew it was appropriate to inform Tony of the allegations that were being made about him and of a possible response from Mr. Rheiner for the killing of his three sons. Yet he didn't know how much he should reveal.

"Jesus Christ, I didn't even know Rheiner had three sons! Hell, nobody did! How could I have killed two men I didn't even know existed? I knew the third son, and I'm glad someone nailed him, but it wasn't me!" The Sheriff was relieved at Tony's reaction because he was clearly angry and surprised. He was usually stoic, totally under control, so the Sheriff took that as an indication that he hadn't commit the murders.

Tony wanted every detail the Sheriff could provide. He was especially interested in the two sons Mr. Rheiner had before he was married.

By the time the Sheriff left, Tony had figured it out. Nearly four years earlier, Tony was hiking along a path on the mountain ridge directly across the valley from where his house was situated. It was near Hyner Point, a popular scenic lookout where he spent many hours during his years at the University. Without warning, he was struck from the side and fell more than thirty feet off a vertical cliff. Although he was badly injured, he survived and was convinced that he had been attacked by a huge man. Yet it happened so quickly that he never saw his attacker. When he reported the incident the Sheriff dismissed it, saying it was probably a black bear. He told Tony that female black bears become very aggressive and unpredictable when they have cubs nearby.

Tony didn't buy the explanation. A few days later his worst suspicion was realized. A large foul-smelling man with a knife emerged from the forest and attacked him. It was the same man who had attacked him earlier. He survived the second attack only because he was able to defend himself with a steel dig bar that was close by. Rather than report the attack and face the investigation that would follow, he took the body of his attacker into the nearby Dead Indian Swamp and watched it slowly sink into a quicksand pool that looked like a polluted pond.

A short time later he left Pennsylvania and headed west eventually landing in Arizona. Once there he was befriended by an old but physically formidable Native American. Tony and his new friend were both attracted to an area several Native American tribes held sacred. Tony's friend believed it was his responsibility to protect the impressive red rock structures in the area. It was all so similar. One day a large man with a very bad smell about him attacked Tony and his friend as they protected the holy area. Tony had a knife, but the Native American was prepared to defend his ancestral land and insisted it was his responsibility. He killed the man with what seemed like little effort, and the body was dumped into a deep crevice.

It was a mystery Tony had lived with. Now he knew, the two attackers were Mr. Rheiner's sons.

In the midst of darkness there can be light; the day of the wedding arrived. The families of Melissa and Tony arrived along with their many friends. The Senator and his Cousin were invited. The Senator couldn't make it, but sent a case of Irish whiskey which his Cousin delivered along with the Senator's best wishes. George was disappointed. An interview with the Senator would have resulted in an increase in the circulation of his newspaper. FBI agents and Crime Commission officials parked at the entrance to the property and took photographs of those who attended. George reciprocated by photographing them and asking them questions. It made an interesting piece in his paper the next day.

Security was on hand to keep out unwanted guests and spectators. Realizing that crime figures would attend the wedding, a Harrisburg newspaper sent two reporters. They foolishly tried to sneak in from the north by walking along the edge of the swamp. They walked past the *No Trespassing* signs and were quickly stopped by armed security. George photographed them and watched as security took their camera and shoes. They were told to "watch for snakes" when they were escorted off the property and left inside the swamp. Their camera and shoes were mailed to them the following day. Sheriff Marsit wasn't happy with the way they were treated, but knew it could have been worst.

Father Callahan was happy to perform the ceremony. He looked beyond his objection to marrying Melissa because of her divorce. Like other priests before him, he could no longer enforce Church rules that were generated by men, not God, and had little to do with the realities of life. He also realized that his behavior, especially in regard to Paula Mary, was far beyond the official teachings of his Church.

The reception was what one would expect when an Irish woman and an Italian man married. Beer, wine and Irish whiskey were consumed in sufficient quantities to produce embarrassing moments that would be regretted the next day and remembered for years.

Melissa's sister Carol had broken up with her boyfriend so she could embrace the excitement that seemed to be everywhere, especially in her new job as a reporter for George's newspaper. She was attracted to powerful men and before long Carol was dancing with the Senator's Cousin. A few drinks, another dance and then a slow walk into the forest along one of the pathways south of the house, away from the swamp. Before leaving the reception, the Cousin approached George with a proposition. "How would you and Carol like to become part of the official press pool that travels with the Senator?"

He was making a name for himself in the world of journalism, and this would surely increase his stature and that of his paper, so George immediately said, "Yes."

Weddings are often times to remember, and not just for the bride and groom. Johnny Boy also made a promising connection during the reception. Doctor Anita Williams, Professor of Literature, was Melissa's favorite faculty member when she was a student at the University. Melissa remained in contact with her after she graduated and they had become friends. The Professor was delighted to attend the wedding and reception, and she quickly came to Johnny's attention. Having taught a course titled "Famous Irish Writers," she and Johnny discovered they had much in common. Her interest in Johnny grew when she discovered he could speak the old language of Ireland—Irish Gaelic. And when she learned that Johnny knew the Senator, she was impressed. Like many young women, she was fascinated by the Senator and his entire family.

THE UNIVERSITY

⬥

Lock Haven was a small town with a very large University. The number of students attending the University was roughly the same as Lock Haven's population, so it wasn't surprising that the economy of the town and the entire county of Clinton was almost entirely dependent on the University. The President of the University was well aware of its importance and was hired not for his academic abilities, but for his perceived business know-how. As soon as he was hired he took major strides to bring in more money and enhance the reputation of the institution. Although far from complete, a research center, new sports facilities and several satellite campuses were all initiated during his first two years. And he knew how to control the internal dynamics of the University so there were no distractions. Public image meant everything and before long the faculty and staff got the message. "The only rule is there are no rules," was a long-standing unwritten dictum within the University to which was added, "The only unacceptable behavior is going public with unacceptable behavior." This was not to say that the President and Board of Trustees would tolerate criminal activity, violence or sexual harassment. It was understood, however, that such behavior had to be reported to them so they could decide if it deserved action by an outside agency.

Professor Williams knew the University planned to open a satellite campus in Wellsboro, a small quaint nearby town known for its gas street lights. She was pleasantly surprised to receive an invitation to the cocktail party that would follow the official ceremony because faculty members were rarely invited to such events. Administrators, board of trustee members and community leaders usually monopolized the rarefied air surrounding University activities. Johnny escorted her and was happy to see that his friend George was also there, escorted by Carol. Johnny, with his Irish brogue, tall muscular body and deep green eyes, was always confident and his connection to the Senator had made him a minor celebrity in the area. Professor Williams knew he would be well received by the others at the party. She also knew they were a striking couple.

Although they weren't romantically involved, George and Carol had come to be known as an influential couple that could make things happen. George's newspaper had become a voice that couldn't be silenced or ignored, and the University community, at some level, appreciated that even as it maintained tight control over information flowing from its own internal sources. Not to be outdone by George, Carol knew her reporting and the rumor of her connection to the Senator's Cousin made her a person of growing interest in University circles and all of Clinton County.

People were finishing their last drinks when a man walked up to Professor Williams and extended his arm over her shoulder as if they were good friends. The expression on her face meant she didn't like it. Johnny reacted quickly, instinctively, by taking hold of his hand with a vice like grip and slowly removing it while pulling the man toward him.

"He's my department head," she said softly, hoping to avoid a scene.

Through clinched teeth, Johnny told the man, "Never touch a woman who is mine." Her department head had flirted with her in the past even while his wife was nearby, and Professor Williams didn't like it. She did, however, appreciate Johnny's effort to protect her and even his seeming to claim her.

The next day Johnny told Tony about the encounter with his girlfriend's department head.

"Yeah, I never liked that son-of-a-bitch. He and his lesbian wife think ..."

"What! His wife is gay—I never heard of such a thing."

"Welcome to the United States. They both work at the University and it's considered clever or chic to have that kind of arrangement, especially if you work in higher education. No matter what they do, they'll claim you're picking on them because of their lifestyle. He's just an asshole no matter what his sexual orientation is. So is his wife. What pisses me off about the two of them is they're always after young women, trying to force them into giving sexual favors. He tried it once with Melissa when she was an undergraduate student. His wife also tried; can you believe that!"

"What did you do?"

"I verbally attacked him at lunch in the student union building while his wife and a hundred people watched. Right in his face, I humiliated him. I wanted him to throw a punch, but he wasn't dumb enough to do it."

"You and I should do something about him."

Tony had a strange smile on his face and slowly moved his hand across his jaw. Staring at Johnny he softly said, "How would you like to make some real money with your bomb making know how? After that we'll deal with the asshole."

"Is someone else planning to attack the Senator?"

"No, this has nothing to do with the Senator … on second thought, it could help him. Maybe it doesn't matter, but a friend of mine wants to get even with someone."

"Helping the Senator and money for a bombing—never got money for anything like that."

"It's up to you. It'll be a lot of money with an honest kind of job afterward as a bonus, right here in Lock Haven, which will help you with your lady friend. You're the expert, but I'll help you with the bombing."

Johnny said he needed to think it over. He realized it would be a big step down a narrow road with no way back.

Cosmo DeGalanti trusted Tony, his son Neil, and no others. And he believed in the lessons that history could teach if only they could be understood, On the wall of his office was a plaque with the following inscription:

The Romans became great by killing their enemies,
not by making peace.

Cosmo was determined to influence history. One federal prosecutor seemed to offer a complex means to make it a reality.

Angelo Martinelli was a federal prosecutor in New York City who earned his reputation as a tough guy going up against both Irish and Italian criminal organizations. Although he was viewed with suspicion by some because his parents were born in Italy, his popularity was so broad that both political parties had approached him about running for office in New York State. When the crime war in Cleveland, Ohio exploded on the scene in the 1970s, he was transferred there in the hope of bringing the bombings and shootings to an end. A three-sided war involving Italian and Irish criminals and corrupt union bosses had become widespread, and more than half of those killed were ordinary citizens with no connection to any of the warring camps.

Bombings were of the greatest threat to the public because in nearly every case innocent people were killed by the blast intended for a rival criminal or a union boss. Solving the problem would be a major challenge even for the most gifted prosecutor. Yet for Cosmo DeGalanti, head of a New York City crime family, the crime war in Cleveland was seen as an opportunity.

Although it wasn't widely known, Prosecutor Martinelli not only investigated violent criminals, he was also deeply involved in federal efforts to stop the flow of cigarettes across state lines in order to avoid state taxes, because movement of goods to avoid those taxes was a federal offense. It was a problem with enormous implications for New York, which had one of the highest taxes on cigarettes of any state in the nation. Cigarettes from Virginia, North Carolina and South Carolina were very inexpensive because of low taxes, thus creating an opportunity for criminals to buy cigarettes in any of the three states and sell them in New York. The practice was so wide spread that more than half the cigarettes sold in New York City were illegal, sold at reduced prices because state taxes weren't paid on them.

While Italian criminals were deeply involved in the sale of untaxed cigarettes in New York, they weren't the only ones who benefited from the practice. The Senator's father was in bed with the Italian mob and had been for decades—and the assassinations of his two sons didn't change things, at least not for him. He once worked with the mob smuggling whiskey into the United States from Canada and Ireland and had made tens of millions of dollars for his efforts. Ironically, those millions were the foundation of the family's fortune and allowed his sons to get into the nation's best universities and later into politics. A statute of limitations protected the Senator's father from prosecution in regard to the movement of whiskey, but not the movement and sale of illegal cigarettes.

Cosmo believed that killing the Prosecutor would at the very least slow the federal government's effort to stop unlawful cigarette sales. Furthermore, he concluded that no matter how it turned out, he and the other crime family bosses could only come out ahead. Helping the Senator in his quest to become President was a favor given today that could be cashed in later, even if the Senator had nothing to do with killing the Prosecutor. Just as the Senator's efforts to become President could be compromised by any suggestion that his father was involved in illegal activities or connected with Italian criminals, the slightest hint that the same criminals eliminated a prosecutor to benefit the Senator would kill the Senator's hope to become President. It was a complex array of players and events that Cosmo believed he could manipulate for the benefit of the crime families. If the Senator were elected President, he would owe the people who helped him. And killing the Prosecutor, Cosmo believed, would benefit the Senator.

When Johnny asked Tony for more information about the killing that required his services, he was surprised at the response, "The guy you're going to kill is investigating the Senator's father. If he goes public with what he's doing, or even worse, if he actually charges the father with a crime, the Senator's chances of ever becoming President will vanish! Kill him and the investigation against the father will die or be delayed until after the election."

Johnny was convinced. Hearing of the many bombings that had taken place in Cleveland during the previous year, he was suddenly eager to move forward. One more bombing in the midst of so many would produce a crime that lacked a clear-cut motive and would have a wide array of suspects from Italian, Irish and union circles.

As was done for the bombing in New Jersey, dynamite sticks, blasting caps and garage remote control units were collected. An automobile was also needed to hold the bomb. A *junk yard* in Luzerne County had plenty of old cars that had been discarded over the years. There was no paperwork on the vehicles and the owner of the yard sold them on an *as is* basis for a flat fee. The buyer simply selected a *junker,* paid the fee and hauled it off. Tony also removed an old Pennsylvania license plate from another vehicle. Tony and Johnny spray painted the car to make it look presentable; attached the license plate; installed a new battery and spark plugs; filled up the gas tank; and started it up without a key, a method often used by auto thieves known as *short wiring.* It wasn't much, yet the automobile ran well enough to get it to the site once it was in Cleveland. The car was loaded onto a flatbed truck and covered with a tarp, making it less likely it could be later identified.

Once in Cleveland, Johnny was on his own. Locating Prosecutor Martinelli was easy because he worked in the federal building in downtown Cleveland. He lived with his wife and son in an apartment building a few miles from his office and parked his car in the enclosed garage area below the apartments. He could be seen from a safe distance coming and going to his car, but there was another problem. If the blast took down a supporting beam, apartments above it would collapse resulting in far more deaths than Johnny was willing to risk. Johnny's bombs often produced explosions and physical destruction far greater than he expected. He wasn't an engineer, so he didn't know what kind of structural damage one of his bombs might generate. That settled it, the bombing had to be done near the Prosecutor's workplace.

Johnny had killed innocent people with a bomb in London. Yet that was exactly what he wanted to do, because they were citizens of Britain, the enemy. Most of them supported their government's continuing aggressive involvement in Northern Ireland, which in Johnny's mind was a war of occupation. Killing the Prosecutor would help the Senator become President of the United States, which would in turn help drive the British from Northern Ireland. That was how Johnny justified what he was about to do. Killing innocent people was immoral, as far as Johnny was concerned, unless every reasonable effort was made to keep them safe.

Two bombs were built with totally different remote-control devices. One was placed in the old car he and Tony had rebuilt. The federal building staff started work at 8 AM, and as usual the Prosecutor arrived early. Johnny was waiting and watching from a safe distance as his target walked at a brisk pace toward the entrance to the building. Suddenly the first bomb, which had been placed in a large public trash container, went off two city blocks away from the Prosecutor. Screams, fire from the blast, people running away from the bombing site ... and the Prosecutor froze momentarily as he looked at the destruction. Before he was a prosecutor he was a police officer, and it was still in his blood. He dropped his brief case and ran toward the destruction in the hope of helping the injured, and toward the old car parked between him and the devastation caused by the explosion. When he reached the old car, Johnny pushed the button on the second remote control. Prosecutor Martinelli was the only person who died.

Johnny had watched it all, and continued watching the result of his work for nearly an hour. Then he took a cab to the bus station. That night he was back in Lock Haven. The next day he had a job as assistant manager of a truck stop outside of Lock Haven, and a brown paper bag filled with twenty, fifty and hundred-dollar bills.

A few days later Lefty, the mob's disabled messenger boy, delivered a verbal communication to Tony. It was from Cosmo, and although Lefty was a trusted member of the family it was *coded*. There were problems with a *friend of the family* who resided in Buffalo, and with a politician in Philly who was making unreasonable demands. The politician refused to be ignored, so not only did he take his demands to the political machine, he also informed mob members knowing they had in the past been deeply involved in presidential politics on behalf of the Senator's family.

Johnny also received an important communication. The Senator's Cousin called and asked to see him. He made it clear he wanted to see him in Lock Haven so he could also talk with George and Carol about future newspaper coverage of the Senator. He told Johnny his wife wouldn't be traveling with him, and that he'd spend two nights in Lock Haven. Johnny understood and said he would give the information to Carol knowing the Cousin had a special interest in her.

KILL THE BASTARDS

———◆———

t was a lively gathering with friends, good food and fine wine. The four couples—Tony and wife Melissa; Johnny and girlfriend Anita; Tony's cousin Joey and wife Samantha; and the Senator's Cousin and Carol—were involved in a lively conversation dealing with politics, especially presidential politics. Should the Senator run for the office of President? When should he announce? Who should be his running mate? What states must he carry in order to win? It caught Melissa's attention when the Senator's Cousin moved his hand from Carol's shoulder to her leg. Melissa gave a nod of disapproval knowing it would have little effect—Carol would be Carol. It wasn't the first time Melissa's sister was involved with a married man. Melissa knew that although the Senator hadn't yet announced his intention to run, Carol would be following his every movement closely, which would place her near the Cousin for months. She also knew it wouldn't end well for her sister.

Dr. Welsh, Anita's boss and the head of the Literature Department at the University, was seated with his wife in the opposite corner of the room. Johnny watched as he stood and moved slowly toward the men's room. When Johnny got up Tony looked at him and said, "Play nice."

Johnny entered the men's room seconds after Dr. Welsh. He grabbed the man who was hated by Anita, Melissa and numerous female faculty and staff members. Johnny pushed him into a toilet stall and held his head in the toilet bowl long enough to make his point. "If you even go near my woman or Melissa again, I'll cut off your balls and feed them to your wife." Johnny was all smiles when he returned to the table. Dr. Welsh stumbled from the restroom and quickly left the restaurant. Johnny fit in nicely with Tony's circle of friends.

Before they left the restaurant, the Cousin took Tony and Johnny off to the side and described what was believed to be another threat to the Senator's life. Two friends of the Westie that Johnny had killed with the assistance of Father Callahan, were shopping for explosives and detonators in the New York City area. Fortunately, what they were seeking wasn't readily available in the City. It was also clear they had never made a bomb before.

The Senator and his father had friends in many places, including the New York City Police Department. Intensive police work resulted in a determination that some of the Westies were going to seek revenge for the murder of their friend. Since the friend had been helping the Senator's Cousin at the time of his death, the police passed on the information they had to the Senator and his father. The Senator figured it out and once again told his Cousin to take care of it. They weren't certain the bomb the Westies were planning to build was meant for the Senator, yet he couldn't take any chances. The Senator was especially concerned that a bomb meant to kill him could very easily kill or seriously injure members of his family. He also reasoned that no one would pay much attention to the killing of two more criminals, something that was taking place with increasing frequency in New York City, Philadelphia, Cleveland and even in Boston.

Tony wanted the Senator to be aware of the violence that had taken place on his behalf. He realized, however, that telling the Cousin something didn't necessarily mean he would pass it on to the Senator. Although he was forced to deal with the Cousin, he didn't trust him. Tony told him that there were two other individuals they needed to confront, although it might be possible to deal with them using a response less drastic than murder. A vicious mobster in Buffalo whose father was imprisoned as a result of investigations undertaken at the direction of the Senator's dead brother, hated the Senator and his family with a passion. He was actively engaged in a range of activities, mostly illegal, to prevent the Senator from becoming President. Then there was a member of the House of Representatives out of the Philly area who demanded a significant sum of money in exchange for his full support of the Senator. He had been paid a substantial amount of money to deliver a huge Afro American turnout when the Senator's brother was elected President, and without that the Senator's brother could have lost in Pennsylvania. The Congressman knew it and was demanding far more money this time, believing the Senator couldn't say no.

The Cousin said he didn't care what they did with the mobster. "Deal with him in any way you wish. Just take care of it, and don't tell me about it. Same thing with the Westies—just take care of them. The Congressman from Philly, now that will take some finesse. We can't spend that much money on a state we thought was a solid win, and we also don't want to offend the Congressman. Stay away from him, and no matter what, don't confront him or his family. I'll take care of it."

The Cousin turned to leave, but Tony stopped him. "There's something else you should know. We, Johnny and I, took care of that federal prosecutor."

Speechless for a moment, then the Cousin exploded, "What! You two did that! Why in God's name did the two of you kill a fucking federal prosecutor?"

"Because he was investigating the Senator's father for shipping cigarettes illegally into New York State. If he filed charges, or even if it just leaked out to the media, the Senator would be done."

"I know nothing about the father's activities; and I'll bet the Senator doesn't know anything about illegal cigarettes. Who in the hell told you?"

"You aren't the only one with sources inside law enforcement. Don't tell the Senator, and if you don't believe me about the cigarettes, just ask the Senator's father," Tony answered.

The Senator and his Cousin often worried that the father would do something to damage the Senator's reputation, in spite of his advanced age—the man was in his eighties. The Cousin knew he had made a lot of money over the years working with Irish and Italians criminals. And although the father was at an age when you wouldn't expect it, he still associated with prostitutes. He even brought them into his home while family members were present.

"Is there any way the death of the prosecutor can be traced back to either of you?" the Cousin asked.

"Not a chance," Johnny answered with a bit of pride.

The Cousin regained his composure and left the restaurant hand in hand with Carol. The others followed close behind and were surprised to see they couldn't wait to get back to the motel. They thought they were put of sight, but they weren't. His hands were up her blouse as they leaned against the car. Melissa screamed at her sister, "Carol, you're like a dog in heat! God how I hate to admit you're my sister."

Tony escorted Melissa to their car and told her, "A little uncontrolled passion between a man and a woman isn't a bad thing." He placed his hand on her inner thigh and she quickly pushed it away.

Tony and Johnny traveled to the Hell's Kitchen area of New York City in search of the two Westies who were looking for bomb building materials. They were surprised at how open and brazen the Westies were about their criminal behavior. Robberies, loan sharking and even past murders were openly discussed on the streets as long as the people of the area believed you weren't a cop. When it came to the Westies, there was both widespread fear and pride. They had successfully confronted the much larger Italian mob, and on a regular basis they outwitted the police.

Tony and Johnny easily identified the two Westies they were looking for. They had a background in loan sharking, robbery and auto theft, and as expected, no experience building a bomb.

The two hung out at a bar on the north side of Hell's Kitchen. Tony was somewhat uneasy about entering the place but Johnny looked, acted and sounded Irish so he figured it would be OK. Introductions weren't necessary if you offered to buy a drink. And after a second drink they behaved as if they were all longtime friends. "All right, I doubt that a Wop and a Dublin Mucker could be cops. Now tell me, what the fuck do you two want from us, here in an Irish bar?"

"We're looking to sell some stuff and maybe even sell some talent ...

I'm from Northern Ireland and I know a thing or two about bomb making … for a price, of course."

"If you're a cop, you ain't a good one, cause this would-be entrapment … Now that's a word I don't often use, but I know it when I see it. So, this better be good."

"Good, aye … that it tis," answered Johnny, with a bit of Irish bluster. "Tis very good, if youse got the gold."

"How much?"

"Five thousand for the finished product, with a one hundred percent warranty!"

"I want a bomb to blow up a goddamn car, I don't need a fucken atomic bomb. How about two thousand for a bomb?"

"How about four thousand for two bombs, because you'll need two if you're going to do one car."

"Two! How in the hell do you figure that?"

"The first is a test, to show you how it works and to see if you like it … to see if it's big enough."

"Huh, a test and to show us … Never thought about it that way. When can you deliver?"

"As soon as you have the money."

"Tonight then."

They gathered in the Bronx in an open area with more than twenty abandoned cars and trucks. It was known as Fort Apache, an area that was lawless except for a block or so around the police station.

"Why only one bomb?" the Westie asked. "I've got the cash for both of them."

"Not so fast. This is the test. If it's OK the next one will be exactly the same. If it's too big or too small …"

"I get it, you'll adjust."

Tony collected the payment for one bomb while Johnny gave a detailed description about how the bomb should be installed and later detonated. "How far do you think you'll be from your target?" He asked the Westies.

"Huh … not sure. Guess it's important or you wouldn't ask."

"Does the target have protection? … Do you care if you kill other people? … Do you want to kill one guy or a group?"

"Yeah, one guy, and he'll probably have protection. Don't care if we get them too."

"Got to watch targets with protection. The protection may be smart enough to spot a suspicious car, or box, or wherever you hide the bomb."

"Hey guys," Tony inserted, "for a price we'll do the job for you."

"Nah, I don't think so. This is kinda personal; I wana see it happen. The bastard hired one of our friends and he ended up in with the garbage. The son-of-a-bitch who wacked him didn't even tell anybody that something happened to him."

"All right then, let's go through this." Johnny said, and then began to show the Westies how to hide a bomb in a car so that it would take out the target. Gas tank full of fuel added to the destruction and additional gas in containers inside the car added extra punch. Explosive materials were expensive, gasoline was cheap.

They moved back to the protection of a second abandoned car. "Get down behind the car and cover your head. Don't look directly at the blast; something can fly from the blast back at you and blind an eye, especially when we're this close … When we're ready, I'll hand you the transmitter. Don't touch the buttons until I tell you."

The four men crouched down behind the vehicle. The two Westies were in the middle. Johnny handed one of them the transmitter. "Look down at the box and cover your head."

Johnny put a bullet in the head of one Westie and Tony took care of the other. They stood up to leave and Tony asked, "What about the bomb?" Johnny laughed a little before saying, "Leave it, it's just junk."

It was too early for the Senator to formally announce his intention to seek the Office of President. Yet he, his Cousin and the press pool were making almost daily trips to colleges and universities; large government facilities including military bases; and large manufacturing facilities. Officially it was all for the purpose of *fact finding*, although hardly anyone believed that. The Senator was planting seeds for the election.

Every visit to a college or university included efforts to form a political action group, an important assignment given to his Cousin.

The Senator's visit to Lock Haven was a major event in the University's history. If the Senator became President, the visit would be recalled for generations; that's how important it was. Coincidentally, the Senator's visit would take place the same day Michael, Tony's oldest son, would be confirmed during a church service that the local bishop would attend. It was a milestone in the life of a family member, and the Martinos loved hosting large celebrations at their mountaintop home. With Tony's Italian family and Melissa's Irish family, there was a tendency to invite *everyone*. The Senator; his Cousin; Italian mobsters; University faculty and staff; and many friends and family members were invited for what was certain to be a gala event. There was a major concern, however.

Tony believed it would be awkward if the FBI and Crime Commission parked their cars at the entrance to his property and photographed people as they entered. He told Sheriff Marsit to inform them that the Senator would be visiting his home in recognition of a Roman Catholic religious event, the confirmation of his son. The Senator wouldn't be happy if the event was compromised by people in law enforcement harassing a family gathered in recognition of a solemn event. Sheriff Marsit got the message loud and clear and passed it on knowing it would have the desired effect. The FBI and Crime Commission played politics and knew it wouldn't be wise to piss off someone who could become President.

The Senator spoke to a large gathering of enthusiastic supporters late in the morning and afterward traveled to Tony and Melissa's home. He was warmly received by the guests and then gave Tony's son a small bible as a confirmation gift. He said he couldn't stay very long but he wanted to speak with Johnny and Tony before leaving. His Cousin joined them and they sat around the kitchen table. "I want to express my sincere gratitude to you Johnny, and to you Tony, for all the help you have provided. My Cousin has kept me abreast of the many obstacles the two of you have overcome. With your continued support and the support of others, I'm sure I'll succeed and carry to new heights the torch my oldest brother once held." Then he spoke the words both men were waiting for. "Once elected, I shall not forget those who helped me achieve the highest office in the land. Johnny, you may convey that to our friends in Ireland. And you Tony can, discreetly of course, inform your friends."

Tony and Johnny were shocked that the Senator had so openly acknowledged their efforts, even in private, with just the four of them present. The Senator continued. "I've directed my Cousin to supply the two of you with all the financial support you request. Finally, is there anything I can do for either of you?"

Johnny immediately answered, "Yes, my lady friend would like to have her photograph taken with you. I know Tony's wife would also like a picture taken with you."

With a slight laugh the Senator replied, "I would be delighted."

The photographer who worked for George's newspaper was already taking pictures and knew the Senator would be in demand for a few. Using the magnificent oak tree as a backdrop, the two photographs were taken. Then a surge of women, some with their children, came forward. The Senator knew how to count votes, so he posed, shook hands, kissed babies and basked in the limelight. He didn't care that he would be late for his rallies at the institutions of higher learning in the Scranton-Wilkes Barre area of Pennsylvania. The Senator and his Cousin had left along with most of the guests when George approached Carol hoping to speak with her about coverage of the Senator. He placed his hand on her shoulder and she winched as if in pain.

"What's wrong, Carol?" When she turned, he saw a bruise on her neck that had been covered until she turned her head. "Where'd that mark come from?"

"It's nothing. I fell and hurt my back and arm." The expression on her face meant there was more to it.

"Did that son of a bitch slap you around?"

"No, no, it was nothing like that. I fell."

"Bullshit! That's why you're all covered up." Then he noticed her eye. "Oh God, you have it all covered up with makeup. I can still see what's left of a black eye. I'll kill that bastard. Just because he's the Senator's Cousin …"

"It wasn't him. I stopped seeing him shortly after we got together, and it won't happen again! I promise, it won't happen again, and don't tell Tony. You know him, he'd do something!"

George insisted she identify the man who hit her, but she refused. She would only say who it wasn't—it wasn't the Cousin of the Senator.

"You're off the Senator's tour. You're still my employee and I'm not going to …"

Carol pleaded with George and eventually he gave in, warning her that it better not happen again. If it did, she would be off the Senator's tour for good.

She agreed, "OK, OK, and don't tell Tony. God, he might kill someone. And I swear, it wasn't the Senator's Cousin."

The next day George's newspaper had a frontpage story about the Senator's visit to Lock Haven, complete with photos taken at Tony's home. He all but endorsed the Senator, in spite of what had happened to Carol. He was certain the Senator had nothing to do with Carol's injuries and that he wouldn't have looked the other way to protect someone else, not even his Cousin. George believed it had nothing to do with politics, and that the Senator was a decent man often embarrassed by those around him, including members of his own family.

Melissa was still tingling at the thought the future President of the United States had visited their home. She instructed Tony to have a stone monument prepared to mark the event. "Place it at the base of the oak tree," she told Tony.

Johnny and Tony hoped that the killings were over. Yet they still had to do something about the mobster from Buffalo, New York who was doing his best to stop the Senator from becoming President. Mario Santucci was involved in unions, politics, construction and crime, and he hated the Senator and his family. Because he was well respected in upper New York state, Mario was capable of moving a large number of votes. New York had been considered a safe state for the Senator, but if one well known Italian turned hard against him others might follow.

Hoping to show his peaceful intent, Tony decided to visit Mario at his place of business and made it part of a vacation—a four-day trip to Niagara Falls. Melissa, his cousin Joey and wife Samantha traveled with him.

After checking in at the Falls-View Hotel on the Canadian side of the Falls, Tony and Joey left the women behind and backtracked to Buffalo, a one-hour drive.

The three of them sat around a table in Mario's office and he immediately told them how he felt about the Senator. "It's because of his family that my father is rotting in jail. We helped his brother become President and then he screwed us! My father, a good Catholic, worked hard to get him elected and then the federal government came after us. They never did it before he was elected, not like that. Funny, isn't it, they sort of left us alone after the President was shot. Now you're telling me to help his brother get elected—the two of you must be crazy."

Joey sat stone faced as Tony tried his best to be diplomatic, something entirely new to him. "I understand your point of view. I felt exactly the same way a few months ago, but not now. We have an arrangement this time. The Senator himself told me we'd benefit after he's elected. I can't tell you the details, but there are good hard reasons why he won't be able to renege on his promise to us."

"Why don't you just kill the son-of-a-bitch? Don't tell me you don't know how to do it—I know about you, and the person sitting next to you."

"I know there's rumors, but ..."

"Rumors, my ass! You and your cousin have killed more men then Jesse James. But you don't scare me, because you can't touch me. That's why you're here all polite and playing nice with me. Killing me wouldn't go down easily with the politicians, the FBI and a lot of our friends, yours and mine, in the City."

"Set killing aside. I don't do that and we don't do it. I'm a businessman here on behalf of other businessmen ..."

"Cut the crap. You're a crook like me. Like the people who sent you here to hassle me. Well it ain't goanna work!"

"Listen Mario, you've got to stop pressuring unions to hold back their support of the Senator; and you must stop promising money to men not to vote …"

"Why? I'm a goddamn American, I have a right to …"

"No, you don't! Some of that is actually a federal crime. Pressuring unions, giving money to potential voters to not vote, to not make telephone calls, to not knock on doors for the Senator—at least some of that is a violation of federal voting laws."

"Yeah, yeah, all small stuff. Politicians do it all the time. You can't kill me and you can't stop me."

"Maybe not, but we can hurt your family and your bottom line."

"My family! What the fuck are you talking about Martino? My kids are clean; they've never been arrested or even investigated."

"True, because you know the system and with your help they stayed below police radar. Moving Cuban cigars makes a lot of money. I know, because I've done it; but it is illegal!"

"Nobody cares. The police don't care. Hell, we sell to lots of cops on this side of the border. On the Canadian side, we just buy them off."

"Sure, but with a little bit of pressure on the police that would change."

"That's low, even for you Martino. But our friends in the City won't want you ratting on me. Hell, they get a cut of my Cuban cigar action."

"And when you and your kids are in jail, they'll get a cut from whoever picks up the pieces. I'll bet my cousin Joey would be happy to play that role, and he would even increase the payments to the families."

"Damn right, I would. I'll even move other stuff to Niagara Falls and go up to Toronto and Ottawa. They're ripe for gambling and other hot merchandise."

Mario didn't have an answer. He just shouted, "Get the fuck outa here, you Wop bastards."

They left after Tony gave him one last piece of advice. "Think it over Mario. Joey and I will be back in a few days. Think about what's best for you, your business and your family. And that killing stuff—Joey and I don't do it, it's all rumors. But if you piss off the Senator and he loses the election; the Irish have killers his people can turn to, like the

Westies. Not the Senator, he wouldn't do it, but his friends just might. Think about that for a goddamn minute."

Four days later Tony and Joey returned and found Mario in a more reasonable mood. "All right, I'll consider it, even helping that bastard in the election. But I get a couple things in return."

"You don't have much room to bargain, Mario … So what the fuck do you want?" Tony replied.

"If the Senator makes it to President, I want him to reduce my father's sentence. He can do it for humanitarian reasons; my father has a bad heart. You got to admit that I deserve that, and so does my father. If you can't deliver that there's nothing we can do with anything else. So, put up or shut up!"

"All right Mario, that's sounds reasonable to me. I'll promise you this: I'll talk directly to the Senator about it. I promise you that. But it can't go anywhere unless he's elected, so just trust me that I'll do it."

"Trust you. I know, I know, that's the way it needs to be done. To tell the truth, even I'll admit he has the inside track. I don't know of anyone who can beat him. But there's more. I want Niagara Falls and all of English Canada. Not really all of it, just the province of Ontario."

"That's asking a lot, and there's already someone in Niagara Falls."

"It's not a lot. There's a family in French Canada out of Montreal, but nothing in all of Ontario. And I'll kick ten percent back to the City's families and three percent to the Martino family. That would move you and your family into the big time. But you'll need to work for it."

That got the attention of both Joey and Tony. It would more than double the income of the Martino family. Yet there were problems. "There's already a family in Niagara Falls."

"Yeah, but their people ain't happy. If the City gives the green light, they'll flip to me without a single body dropping. I'm an earner, a money maker. The guys in the trenches up the road in Niagara Falls know me. They'll come to me in a heartbeat and the bosses there will cave in. All I need to do is buy them out. Hell, they're old and ready to cash in their chips so they can get outta New York and go live in Florida."

"I like it, but I can't approve it on my own. I'll pass it on to the families and see what they think."

"Yeah, yeah, but what do you think? I know who you really are Martino. I know what you really do. Lots of people think you're that so called Lone Wolf killer, *Lupo Solitario*, that's been talked about for four or five years, and I'm pretty sure they're right. I know the families won't listen to me, I've tried. But if you present the idea and back it, they'll pay attention. They'll listen to a guy like you."

Tony quietly considered the proposal. Mario added, "And that three percent to the Martinos is a lot of money, so you'll be a hero back home. After the City backs my idea, all you need to do is help me move Cuban cigars in Pennsylvania. And if I need it, supply some muscle in my territory."

"Let me think about this for a minute."

Mario knew he was interested, so he wanted to close the deal. "In the spirit of cooperation, and because you're no good to me if your dead," Mario laughed, because he couldn't help himself. "I'll tell you something that could save your life or long jail time. Not just for you, for your whole family."

"You're nuts!"

"Nuts, am I? I know the FBI is looking at you real close because of all the killings around you. And they came up with two things that can hurt you or bring down our family."

"Like what?"

"First, my sources ain't perfect, but I'm told there's at least one guy, maybe two, who aren't in your family, they're Capilanos, who's talking to the FBI. Maybe the FBI's talking more to them, than they are to the FBI, but they are talking! FBI agents are telling them if they produce information to bring down the Martinos, the Capilanos will be protected. Then the Capilanos will have everything."

"That doesn't make sense. There's no way to bring us down without hurting the Capilanos. Besides, the FBI would never stick to the deal. They'd go right after the Capilanos after they hurt us."

"Eh, I didn't say the guys doing the talking are smart. I just said they're talking and listening. And it might be just one guy. The feds know that the Martinos beat the hell out of one guy at some meeting and then his girlfriend dropped him. The FBI told him the Martinos told her to get rid of him. The guy must not be smart, and the FBI is trying to use the beating to turn him. So, I'm just telling you what my sources told me. Does any of it hold water?"

Joey and Tony knew exactly who he was talking about. "Yeah, some of it could be true. But why would someone inside the FBI tell you?"

"For the same reason FBI agents in Boston are in bed with the Irish mob. They even helped the Irish commit murder and helped the head of the group leave Boston and disappear like a ghost in the wind. Money buys friends, even with the FBI."

"You said the FBI had two things to hurt me and my family. What's the second thing?"

"It's also about revenge, but from a non-Italian. This guy claims you killed his three sons."

"I heard about that. The FBI thinks he may try to get me, but he's afraid of how my family would react, and he should be."

"See that, my sources are good, ya gotta admit it. Now this seems screwy, but here goes. The FBI told him he'd be protected if he did kill you."

"I find that hard to believe."

"Really? If he tries to kill you, hit or miss, there'd be a reaction from your family that the FBI would be ready for. They'd jump into the chaos with information from the informant and bring down the entire Martino family while it's distracted going after the guy who's trying to wack you, or maybe he gets lucky and gets you. During that time, they'd protect the informant and his family. It's illegal as hell, but that never stopped the FBI. Don't forget, the FBI was always for the Irish and against us. You need to worry about attacks coming your way from two directions: the FBI using an informant against you and your family, and an attempt to kill you coming from the outside."

"Why are you telling me all of this?"

"Oh yeah, now we're getting to it, ain't we?"

"So why?"

"The last time you two were here, after you left I thought about all of it for a long time. I figured I'm either all in or all out. If I'm out, the Senator will come after me if he becomes President … and if I'm out, I pissed off the families and the two of you. I run the risk of going to jail or getting wacked. So, I figure I gotta be all in. That means keeping you alive and out of jail. Yeah, and it also means you've gotta do the same for me—Capeesh?"

Tony nodded and Joey was also satisfied, especially with the money that would be coming the Martino family's way.

"So now the two of you gotta do your part—go kill the bastards!"

ANOTHER WAR?

C osmo DeGalanti was furious when he learned another FBI informant had penetrated the ranks of his organization. Learning it was a Capilano, he shouted, "We should have killed all of the goddamn bastards three years ago when they tried to change things. We were easy on them and they do this. Do what you must Tony, to get rid of this traitor!"

"Listen Pop," his son replied, "I told you once before that you can't just give Tony a free pass to start killing. For Christ's sake, you never know where it'll end!"

"End! End! … You're my son, but you're soft." Giving in only slightly, he added, "You're smart Tony, so think before you do anything. But know this, it will be on you and my stupid son if this rat goes too far. Just take care of the goddamn Capilano rat, whoever it is. One other thing, you go back to the hard coal region and tell everyone that your father now represents my interests there. I no longer trust a Capilano to run things—Capeesh?"

"Yeah, I know what it means, but putting my father in charge of everything …"

"Anybody don't like it, whack them!"

Number one and number two within the hard coal crime family had suddenly changed places, something neither of them was entirely happy about; especially since they needed to find the informant and eliminate the possible threat he posed.

Frank Martino along with Tony and Joey represented their family's interests while Jake Capilano stood alone against them. "Listen guys, I know we'd all be hurt by an FBI squealer. But we gotta be careful so we don't nail the wrong guy or piss off a lot of my people."

Frank wasn't big on waiting. "If we kill five or six Capilanos the rest will get the point, including the traitor, if he ain't one of them we got."

"Be reasonable, Frank. Do that and we'll have another war and …"

"If we kill your five best, there can't be a war. You won't have any real men left."

"I hear you, no good men to do killing, but there will be fifty or sixty other guys who might take up the fight. Even if they never did a killing before, they may be angry enough to try."

"Not if you tell them to stand down," Tony inserted. "And tell them with some force behind it. Then only one or two reckless guys will try anything, and we'll cut them off at the knees and kill some of their family for good measure."

It was a bleak picture, yet Jake suspected he could reach a painful compromise. "Listen Tony, I know you don't want to kill family members. Hell, some of them are your friends or family of friends." Turning his attention to the father he added, "Besides, there must be other things we can do besides killing."

"Don't know, but killing the guy who turned against us is …"

"OK Frank, I get it, and that's just one guy to eliminate. I can live with that, but we have no idea who it is."

Joey finally spoke up. "I can pick out six of your guys and I'd be pretty sure it's one of them—Tony and me know all the ones who hate us Martinos."

"Joey's right," Frank replied. "I know you don't want to kill six to get one. But things like that have been done before, and you know it. Just start with six guys you think are most likely and work from there, Jake."

"Give me time and I will."

"Time, there's the rub. Give you time and we give the FBI and their guy in your family time to screw us. Time has costs to it."

"I'll do everything to find the guy as fast as I can."

"Damn right you will, because it's going to cost you a lot of scratch right up front—about a million dollars to buy time."

"What in God's name are you talking about, Frank."

"You're going to sell me a million in real estate for a hundred thousand. That's how you're buying time; ten cents on the dollar. Find the son-of-a-bitch in two weeks and I'll return half to you for ten cents on the dollar."

"Jesus Christ, I'll be busted!"

"No, you won't. Squeeze your guys for a share of the money and tell them why—that'll get their attention."

"That could drive another guy to the FBI."

"Not when you hear the rest. Tell them there's an FBI rat in your family and when we identify him ..."

"I know, you'll kill him."

"No, much more. We'll go after every one he loves: wife, children, mother, father and girlfriend, if he's got one. The FBI can protect him, but not everyone else, even his friends ... If the FBI tries to hide all of them, it'll be impossible—we'd find some of them. Just tell your guys that."

"Holy Christ, Frank, even the families from the City wouldn't go along with that."

"They already have," Tony answered.

"Just so you know Jake, and you can tell your guys. I'll use the money I get from you to hire men in advance to do the work—men from outside of Pennsylvania. When the first Martino is arrested by the FBI, maybe even just called in for questioning, the informant will probably be known. Then his family starts getting knocked off. Outsiders will start killing until they use up the money you're fronting me."

"You're gonna use my money to kill my family!"

"Yeah, seems fair to me. It's your family talking to the FBI, and it could end up putting my family in jail—I take that real personal. I'll tell you something else, the City families will be coming at you personally, if one of yours talks to the FBI."

It seemed like the wrong thing to do—tell the Capilano family that the FBI had penetrated it, and the informant was placing all Capilanos at risk. In the short run, it meant Jake and other members of the family would suffer financially. But it would put them on notice and then they would be expected to *police* each other. Almost immediately, however, the strategy seemed to produce results. Two of the six men Frank Martino believed were most likely to cooperate with the FBI began to move their family members out of hard coal country. Guilty or not, it was what the informant would do to protect those most dear to him. Yet both men appeared to have legitimate reasons for their actions. The mother-in-law of one lived in Arizona and had a stroke. Her daughter and their children moved there to care of her. The daughter of the other man lived in South Carolina and was in the midst of a heated legal battle involving custody of children and distributions of assets following a divorce. Frank Martino wasn't making life easy for Jake and even suggested that both men could be FBI informants. Jake knew what that meant. If the informant wasn't identified soon, Frank would direct that both men be killed. Fortunately, an additional piece of information came from an unlikely source: a cop.

Sheriff Marsit owed Tony something neither man would ever forget. The Sheriff once beat a young man after stopping him for drunk driving. Slapping him around would have been ignored, but he broke the kid's nose, which should have resulted in the Sheriff losing his job. It could have even produced a criminal conviction against the Sheriff. Instead, Tony entered the picture and paid off the young man's father. He sealed the deal by promising to return with a vengeance if the man or his son ever broke the agreement and went public. The Sheriff owed Tony, so when he learned something about a Capilano he passed it on to him.

During a routine stop, a State Police Officer discovered a significant amount of heroin in Danny Capilano's car. Possession of an illegal drug was serious business. Yet weeks after that, charges had still not been filed. The Sheriff knew charges were often dropped against offenders with a clean background, but Danny was no saint. Loan sharking, gambling and assault were written all over his rap sheet, so he was the kind of guy police and prosecutors nailed to the wall. Why didn't it happen in his case? Tony thought he knew the answer—the FBI stepped in to help Danny in exchange for information. At least that's what Tony believed. Tony told Frank, but Frank still wasn't completely certain. And Frank wanted that: absolute certainty! Still believing it might be wise to kill both men to completely eliminate the possibility of an FBI informant doing any damage, Frank told Jake to set it up: immediately bring in both men for a *face-to-face* knowing at least one them would leave as a corpse.

It was surreal. The two Capilano suspects were brought into the room by Jack Capilano and seated on one side of a table opposite their judge and jury, Frank Martino. Jack sat between them and Jake was the prosecutor. Gun in hand, Tony stood at the door. Then it began.

Jake: Both of you know why you're here. One of you, or both of you, ratted to the FBI. That means someone won't be breathing when they leave here.

First Man: I swear to Christ, it wasn't me!

Second Man: It wasn't me. I know what happens to guys who talk too much.

Jake: Let me lay it out, business like. If you're the one, it will be better for your family if you talk. Then you'll be the only one who gets it. Someday the FBI will release the name of the rat, probably to Tony. Tony has a working relationship with the FBI because of his work with the Senator. If you tell us today then only you get it. If you don't tell us today you both die and then later, when we figure it out, your family gets it—mother, father, sisters, brothers, grandparents, wife and kids. Get the idea? The FBI can hide some of them, but not all of them. And one day you'll be fingered; it's just a matter of time.

First Man: Sobbing.

Second Man: You fucking bastard, tell them! It wasn't me, you're the one. I shouldn't die, you son-of-a-bitch!

Joey: One dead or two, I don't give a shit. Two dead we know the rat got what he deserves. One and we ain't sure.

Frank: Kind of hate this: mother, father, sister, brother and wife all get wacked. Guess the rat figures they deserve to pay for his fucking mistakes.

Frank placed a 38 caliber Smith and Weston revolver on the table along with two bullets. "This was my father's. Funny, he used it for deer hunting. He never shot one, but it'll work just fine today. Huh, one or two bullets, hate to waste any of Pop's bullets. This should take only one."

First Man: Holy Christ! … More sobbing.
Second Man: Screams something unrecognizable.

Frank placed one bullet in his father's revolver.

Jake: Jesus Christ, you two! If we need to kill both of you; you shame all the Capilanos and I'll piss on both your graves.

Frank placed the second bullet in the revolver. "Well Jake, you or me—who does it?"

Jake: "It's my family, I will …"
Second Man: "I swear on my mother's grave, I didn't do it!"
First Man: "It's me, but I didn't say much. Ya don't need to kill me. I swear, it wasn't much! I'll tell the FBI that …"
Frank: "Know what Jake, you shouldn't do it. He should."

Frank pointed at the second man.

Second Man: "Me? I never killed nobody and …"
Jake: "Yeah, you're right Frank. That way he can never testify against us."
Second Man: "I never killed …"
Frank: "Only blood can bring this to an end. Kill, or be killed with the rat. For me, I'd just as soon kill both of you. Still not sure about you anyway. If you're dead, I'd be sure."

Jake moved the revolver. The second man picked it up and fired quickly, hitting his cousin in the neck.

Frank: "There's still another bullet in there—use it!"

The second shot tore away part of the jaw, exposing teeth while body tissue flew across the floor ... Yet the body thrashed around on the floor.

Joey became irritated. "Tony, give me your goddamn knife." He thrust it into the throat ... all movement stopped.

As the Martino's were leaving, Frank looked real hard at Jake. Pointing at Danny Capilano, the second man, he had an *I told you so* look on his face as he spoke. "We nearly killed the wrong guy." Turning to Danny, he continued. "I'm still not sure about you. I still think killing both of you would have been the thing to do. You selling drugs and not being charged; that still bothers me. I want to be very clear about this. If you have any ideas about making deals, look at the body of your cousin over there. It'd be better to serve time than have your family end up like your cousin. Capeesh, Danny?" Danny shook his head.

Jake knew how to get things done. He stood near the cremation furnace until there was nothing left but ashes and the two slugs. They were returned to Frank. The next day the Capilanos had a funeral. It was the right thing to do. There weren't many questions. Everyone who mattered knew what they needed to know. Even the FBI knew.

Like Cosmo DeGalanti, the head of his crime family, Tony knew history and was often inspired by it. He recalled the words of a Native American chief after fighting many battles in the futile war with the white man.

I shall kill no more, forever.

He wondered if he could end his killing ways. He knew Joey couldn't. And his father—killing was how he survived World War Two; it was how he protected his family during their war with the Capilanos; and it was the only way he could deal with the threat an FBI informant had created. He wondered if killing was in his blood the way it was in the blood of Joey, his father and the great predators of the animal kingdom.

Monsignor Lessari was the only priest who had ever heard Tony's confession. Having asked God for forgiveness, Tony always felt morally cleansed when he left the confessional. The Monsignor's words, "Your sins are forgiven ... In the name of the Father, Son and Holy Spirit ... Go forth and sin no more," allowed him to face the world seemingly as a new man.

Could his friend Father Callahan possibly become Tony Martino's confessor? Father Callahan understood killing. During the Korean War, he had killed more often and with greater brutality than Tony had or ever would. Such was the nature of combat.

While receiving the sacrament of confession, even a killer can lay bare his soul. It was an informal confession in his friend's office, yet Father Callahan was morally bound to hold secret everything Tony told him. "Bless me father for I have sinned ..." was how it began; how it began for all Roman Catholics when they asked forgiveness for their sins, great and small. He told the good Father of his many sins and his hope that in the future he would not once again commit the gravest of them. Father Callahan knew exactly how his friend felt, recalling his confession after leaving the battlefields of Korea. Killing armed men came to mind when he recalled his time in Korea. Even killing prisoners of war and civilians seemed at times to be necessary; looking back, he now knew it was not. They were acts of a blood rage that had taken hold of him. Combat medals and citations were given to him for his service and they resulted in guilt, because they were of this world. Nightmares of his spirit followed him in this life and he knew they would stay with him into the next.

For the first time, he felt a true kinship with Tony and believed that by helping him he might in some way help himself.

The past could not be undone. Alfred Rheiner, however, was part of Tony's future—and killing him was not something Tony eagerly looked forward to. Yet Father Callahan understood when through his emotional pain Tony said, "Killing Rheiner may be the only way I can get on with my life. One more and then no more, forever." In his mind he could justify it, but what of his soul?

Father Callahan believed there was another way. He would present Alfred Rheiner with a proposal for peace and he would broker the peace. He would then do everything, lay down his life if necessary, to guarantee it. They had gambled together, drank together and killed a Westie together—and now Father Callahan and Tony Martino would try to move beyond killing together.

Alfred Rheiner was not a fool. For his own sake and for the sake of his remaining son, he agreed to end the conflict that had taken the lives of his other three sons. Although the hate would endure, so too would the peace.

THE ANNOUNCEMENT

———◆———

Carol had the job of her dreams and she was looking forward to the big announcement—the Senator's official statement that he was seeking the Office of President. It was scheduled to take place in two weeks, more than enough time for national and international news agencies to prepare. Carol also needed to prepare for the big event. She had been traveling with the press pool that followed the Senator's every move for more than three months and it had taken its toll. Stress of the job, late nights, too much alcohol and an abusive lover left her feeling exhausted and anxious.

Her boyfriend was married, but didn't have any children. He told Carol he'd divorce his wife and marry her after the election. She knew that was very unlikely and told him so. Yet she treasured their relationship in spite of the violence that he directed at her when he was drunk. He would always apologize afterward, although he took every opportunity to verbally humiliate her, especially making comments about the weight she had gained.

Two weeks wasn't much time, but it was enough for her to recover physically and perhaps emotionally. She returned to Lock Haven to rest and mend knowing her sister Melissa and George, her employer, always had her best interests in mind.

The day after she returned to Lock Haven she saw her physician. Seeing the bruises on her body, Doctor Thompson became angry and demanded to know who had harmed her. Carol knew that could lead to police involvement, something she desperately wanted to avoid. As the physician continued the examination it became clear why Carol was anxious and had gained weight—she was pregnant. Knowing it could dramatically change her life, she didn't tell her boyfriend of her condition hoping the signals her body was sending were false. Knowing she was carrying the child of an abusive boyfriend, her physician's anger grew. "I don't care if he is married. You must tell him you're pregnant, and you should also tell his wife. I know it's not my responsibility to get so deeply involved in a patient's life, but you're so removed from reality that you didn't even realize you're carrying his baby. What on earth is wrong with you?"

Carol was in a state beyond words, beyond shock. She was raised Roman Catholic and was taught that God and the Holy Mother would protect women if they simply had a good heart. Although she had been sexually promiscuous since graduating from high school, she had never harmed anyone. Being pure of heart, which she believed she was, meant that nothing incredibly bad could ever happen to her. Death of loved ones, such as the deaths of her parents, was natural and expected. She understood that and accepted it. But this: an unplanned pregnancy resulting from a relationship with a married abusive lover was incomprehensible to her. Surprisingly, the fact that he was a married man was something she had rationalized away, believing it didn't matter as long as his wife never knew.

When Carol left the doctor's office she was on the verge of mental collapse. Other than confiding in her sister, she didn't know what to do. Should she tell her boyfriend and perhaps even his wife, as the doctor suggested? Should she quit her job and not return to the Senator's campaign trail? Should she have an abortion, or commit suicide and end her life as well as the unborn child's?

Doctor Jill Thompson was also shaken when Carol left her office. She considered informing the police that Carol had been beaten while she was pregnant; and she knew George, Carol's employer, and was certain he'd become furious if he discovered that Carol had been treated so badly. Lock Haven was a small town where people knew a good deal about each other. Doctor Thompson knew Tony, Carol's brother-in-law, by reputation. She heard and believed he was capable of extreme violence and suspected things could become ugly if he learned about Carol's situation. However, she expected that Carol would tell Melissa anyway, which meant that Tony would eventually learn at least as much as she knew. Realizing it was a difficult state of affairs that could easily escalate into an effort to identify and punish Carol's boyfriend, Doctor Thompson decided to "wait and see."

When Carol returned to the mountaintop home of Melissa and Tony, she immediately lost her composure. She told Melissa about her life during the previous three months including her time with her boyfriend. Yet she remained loyal to him in her own way, refusing to identify him. Her commitment to him was so deep that she even said, "It wasn't all his fault … I should have been more careful with him. He drinks a lot, and if I just stayed away from him during those times …"

"Are you crazy!" Melissa shouted. "A man should never do this to any woman, especially one who's carrying his baby."

"I know, I know, but he didn't know I was pregnant … I thought I might be pregnant and I guess I should have told him …"

"It doesn't matter! He's a nasty monster, and when Tony hears …"

"Oh God, don't tell him any of this! He'd kill him! You know that, Tony would just kill him!"

Melissa knew Carol was right. But her sister was pregnant and although it was only three months, she was beginning to show it. How long could they keep it from Tony? And then there was Olga. She was a strong person with a kind heart who seemed to see everything and know everything. Reluctantly, Carol agreed that Olga should be told, rather than having her figure it out on her own.

Strangely, Olga was calm and barely spoke when the sisters confided in her. She even agreed not to tell Tony for fear that he would seek out Carol's boyfriend and kill him. Yet Melissa knew enough about Olga to realize she was in many ways like Tony—deeply devoted to family and willing to go to any length to protect them. And although she wasn't a blood relative of anyone who lived in their mountaintop home, she was in many ways the Russian mother bear who would die to protect her family. Olga was 65 years old, and had fought to defend her county at

Leningrad during World War Two, even as her husband and children were killed by the German war machine. She would do no less to protect her adopted American family.

Hoping to conceal her condition from Tony, Carol decided to move in with a female friend in downtown Lock Haven. She departed before Tony arrived home, and he barely noticed her absence when he did return. Yet she still worked for George's newspaper and he needed to be insulated from the reality of her situation. Fortunately, he was out of town on business for two days, which gave her time to heal and create a cover story.

George was a big man with a booming voice who easily intimidated most people. Also, his growing stature as a newspaper man meant that he was a force to be reckoned with in political circles and in the Lock Haven community. It seemed inconsistent with his outward appearance, but George was generous to a fault and cared about his employees at the newspaper and his bar, Diamond Lil's, far more than most employers.

Seeing Carol after he returned from his trip, George immediately knew that something was wrong. Most of her bruises had disappeared and the rest were concealed with makeup and clothing. Even her pregnancy wasn't apparent because of the baggy clothing she had begun to wear. Yet in spite of her best efforts, George knew she wasn't feeling well.

When she told George, "I'll be fine in a day or two. Then I'll return to the Senator's political tour." He responded by saying, "No, you will not!" George spoke forcefully, but with a faint smile. "You're tired, sort of burned out. Three months on the road did that. Jesus Carol, even your skin color is off. Take some time off to recover here in Lock Haven, and I'll follow the Senator the next few weeks. Besides, I have an interview scheduled with him the day before he's expected to make the big announcement. It's going to be a huge event that the major TV networks are planning to cover."

Carol protested, but she knew he wouldn't change his mind. She also knew he was right.

She needed to stay away from him although the need to talk to her lover was more than she could bear. That night she called him and told him she wouldn't return to the Senator's campaign tour for a few weeks. When she told him she was pregnant, he began screaming at her. Once things calmed down he told her to have an abortion. She didn't agree although she didn't completely rule it out. She also recalled when Melissa considered having an abortion. It was a painful time and in the end her sister had the child. Their conversation ended with him telling her, "I don't need a baby in my life and I'm not even sure it's mine! Damn it Carol, do the right thing and put this behind us. Without a baby, we'll have a good life together."

He was so dishonest that it left Carol in a deep depression with thoughts of suicide. Yet she still wanted to protect her boyfriend and was concerned that Tony would somehow identify and kill him.

Plans for the big announcement had been made months before and it was scheduled for the next day in the lobby of the Benjamin Franklin Plaza. It was one of the largest hotels in Boston and the Senator and his staff occupied the entire penthouse floor. Final preparations and celebrations were going on simultaneously as journalists mixed in with the Senator's staff and family. George arrived and joined in with the festivities, consuming several cans of beer while he waited for the designated time. He met the Senator's wife, two daughters and son. They joked with him about going easy on their father during the interview.

In the midst of the chaos a telephone call came in for George. The Senator's son had taken the call and graciously allowed George to use his office so he could speak to the caller in a quiet area. It was totally unexpected. It was Olga on the other end of the line.

The timing couldn't have been worse. George was still processing Olga's call when he was told the time had come. The interview would be viewed on national television to an audience of millions and George had never conducted a live TV interview. Yet he knew that his interview with the Senator was the first of many scheduled for that day and it would likely be forgotten within hours.

They shook hands on camera and sat across from each other for what was expected to be largely a *soft ball* political event. In keeping with that, George asked questions about the Senator's family and about the historic Boston area. The Senator beamed as he answered each of them. Then George asked, "Why do you want to be President?"

George was shocked at the response to what should have been an easy question. "Well, there are things I want … that we all want, to be sure … which if elected, and I'm sure I'll be elected …"

The Senator's response was rambling and incoherent. George sat quietly as the Senator continued. "As a nation, we must do the correct … things … which a great nation could, no should be able to do …"

For the next few minutes the Senator continued to respond while George sat there speechless. It was so painful George wanted to end the interview, but he didn't know how to do it gracefully. Finally, a red light went on, just off-camera, in an area George could see. It meant time was up for the interview.

George left the Senator not knowing what to do about an interview that made both of them look foolish. Yet George wasn't the one running for President, so after another beer he felt better about the whole thing. He then looked across the room and could tell the interview had changed the mood of family, news people and supporters who had gathered for what was expected to be an historic event followed by hours of merriment. The joy that had filled the air just a short time ago had clearly been replaced with apprehension.

George knew he had to make things right, so he approached the Senator's son and said, "Could I talk to you in your office?" The son agreed and they picked up a six pack of beer before sitting down behind closed doors. The son had expected that George would allow him to somehow enhance the response his father had so completely stumbled over. They sat across from each other with only a small table between them.

George began with a difficult question. "Roe vs. Wade is only a few years old—so how do you feel about abortion?"

The son was ill prepared, but he tried to answer. "As a Roman Catholic, I feel that abortion is morally wrong, which is what my father would …"

"Then how can you tell Carol to kill your baby!"

Suddenly George lunged across the table and grabbed the Senator's son by the throat. George was big, powerful and angry as hell. Once the son fell to his knees, George held his throat with his left hand and smashed his face repeatedly until the jaw was broken, then the nose, and finally the skull was cracked. The son fell to the ground silent and bleeding. Three kicks to the son's side added broken ribs to his injuries.

George was satisfied, but he wasn't finished. He walked to the son's desk and called in two stories to his newspaper. The first was about the Senator's bizarre and incoherent response to a simple question. The second was about his attack on the Senator's son, in which he tried to justify the assault. Both stories appeared on the front page of his paper the next morning. They were quickly picked up and echoed by news organizations around the world.

By the next morning, George was arrested and an air of gloom had fallen over the Senator's campaign. Yet the nation held its breath, wondering what the Senator would do. The room was filled with TV cameras, news media people and his supporters, and they were subdued when he spoke to them.

"My effort to seek the highest office in the land ended yesterday. Yet the torch of justice will not die for all who share our vision of the future. Our hopes will continue in the hearts and minds of millions, and our voices shall never be silenced!"

History is made by great men,
while others record what they are permitted to see.

The End

ACKNOWLEDGEMENTS

At long last, the third installment in the Anthony Martino *hard coal country saga* is complete. The fourth and final novel in the series has been started and will be finished in two years—*God willing and if the creek don't rise.*

Today I write for the joy of it and, as I've said and written many times, "to maintain what is left of my sanity in an insane world." In my previous life, as a professor of engineering and a consultant, I also did a good deal of writing. Although I enjoyed it, it was done to support myself and my family, so there was always something of an urgency about it. The writing I do today serves a far different purpose, and is done in a totally different atmosphere. Writing novels, especially those involving Anthony Martino, is both interesting and incredibly enjoyable, including the interaction it produces with a wide array of family and friends—and then there are my *gym buddies.*

Bill still does my typing and without his help I'd be lost. I simply can not write effectively while sitting at a computer, preferring instead to write at a shopping mall, casino, the beach, or the gym—anyplace there is something interesting taking place in the background. Bill is able to convert my handwritten and somewhat disorganized pages into a computer file, and for that I am grateful.

Marty is still *king of the gym*, a title he bestowed on himself. He is interested in all things Irish, as I am in all things Italian. Italians, of course, make far better food than the Irish and I often remind him of that. He was a useful source of information when I was uncertain about the behavior and descriptions of the Irish characters in the novel.

John and Jack are good guys and are useful participants in the gym banter about Italian criminality, which takes place surprisingly often. It's funny how *Dago Red* always seems to come up in our conversations. Should I be insulted?

Stan *the man* and Judy are newcomers to the gym scene, at least the gym environment I'm involved with. They seem to enjoy my previous books, for which I am grateful, and I suspect they'll also appreciate this one.

Most importantly, Elizabeth Mary, my wonderful wife, is always supportive of my writing and patiently listens as I read the latest revision of a chapter. I often get lost in my writing, but she's always there waiting to welcome me back to reality. For her help, I often reward her with a back massage and my rendition of *I love you a bushel and a peck.*

Thank you God for my family, friends and
a wonderful ever-changing life.

Printed in the United States
By Bookmasters